KASH & HEAVEN

LOVED BY A STREET SAVAGE

BY

NA'COLE

KASH & HEAVEN: LOVED BY A STREET SAVAGE

KASH & HEAVEN: LOVED BY A STREET SAVAGE

KASH & HEAVEN: LOVED BY A STREET SAVAGE

ONE

Seven Months Ago

Sitting a few cars behind Agents Bullock and Hassan, dipped low in the cut, Kash watched them intently. In an all-black Tesla with tinted windows, he placed a tightly rolled, exotic filled Dutch to his slightly darkened lips. With squinted eyes, he took a puff as he pulled his fitted cap down low, allowing a dark cloud of smoke from the Dutch to pervade the car, slightly impairing his vision. This moment felt so damn intense. Kash's heart rate picked up in speed as he anticipated what he was about to do.

Although Lance sat on the side of him, it was as if he wasn't there. Kash was in his zone. He waited on the phone call to come through from Dre so that he could proceed with their plans. He was ready to catch a few bodies. Him getting away with these murders was going to be one hell of an ego trip. Hunting the usual hunters gave Kash an adrenaline rush. His trigger finger was itching, and the trigger he held in his hand was for sure going to leave a gruesome scene.

Blowing dark smoke from his mouth, Kash sighed a deep breath and passed the Dutch to his partner in crime. This cat and mouse game was a little nerve wrecking. Bullock and Hassan really didn't realize just how dangerous the Wright family was, and Dre hiring him to carry out this act was like icing on the cake. Kash took missions like this one seriously. He never did anything of importance mediocrely. He saw the agents' deaths play out in his head, and he heard their ear curdling screams. Kash chewed on his inner jaw, toying with the mini remote he held in his hand. He had nothing personal against either agent. He was simply hired to do a job that paid pretty handsomely. This here was all business. Kash was ready to murk the two agents and move the fuck around.

His entire outfit was black, from his hat to his shoes. So was Lance's. They almost looked like chameleons with the way they blended in with the interior of the self-driving vehicle.

Kash's hair, a sandy brown Caesar fade, was hidden underneath a black, Chicago Bulls, leather fitted cap, and his size thirteen right foot tapped against the black floor mat anxiously. Butterflies fluttered around his stomach every so often, making him feel a little uneasy.

Kash retrieved the Dutch from Lance and took another pull from it. His mind rambled, having an intoxicated conversation with itself. He placed the cigar between his index and middle fingers as he coughed. It was pitch-black outside, and the block was too quiet. It was not an unusual quiet, but the silence made Kash over think.

"Here, G." Through red glazed over eyes, he tried to pass the weed back to Lance. He was starting to feel the effects, and he had to stay focused.

"I'm good, bro." Lance declined.

Kash snuffed the weed out. Staring straight ahead, he sighed, feeling his phone buzz on his lap. Never taking his eyes off the agents, Kash picked up his phone. He pressed talk, and a woman's voice boomed loudly through the receiver.

"Kashmir!" she yelled. "Where the fuck are you? The babies need some milk, and I'm hungry."

Lance couldn't do anything but shake his head and smirk at Kash's interest in certain women.

"I'm busy, Asia," he said in a calm tone. Although Kash was a killer, he had a calm demeanor. His voice was almost never raised in anger. He was a man with patience because he understood that his lifestyle made the women he dealt with feel insecure.

"I got you in a minute when I'm done here."

"You're busy? Busy doing what? Kash, you better not be with no other bitch."

"I'm not," he said shortly, not really wanting to argue with her. He had to watch his surroundings and stay focused on his task.

"Why is your background so quiet, Kashmir?"

"Asia…" He let out a breath. "Let me call you back."

"Nah, fuck that, Kash," she said, yelling. Asia was unbearable at times. They had only been together for about two months now. He didn't even know how they ended up in a relationship. What started off as a few hearts under her pictures on social media quickly turned into him fucking her a few times in the trap, which then led to them talking almost every day. Somehow, a couple of months later, Kash became a family man. With no kids of his own, besides the daughter he never had the chance to meet, Asia quickly claimed him as hers and forced her three kids on him. Kash didn't trip however. He loved kids. He took her six and four year-old daughters, as well as her one-year-old son, in as his own.

"Maaan, Asia, I said let me call you back. Clear my line, shorty," finally, he hung up on her.

"I thought Esha was crazy." Lance chuckled.

"Asia play that crazy role. But she's cool."

"Sounds like she was tryna keep you on the phone long enough to track your location," Lance said seriously. He was suspicious of Asia, mainly because he didn't know her that well. She seemed kind of clingy and psychotic.

"She ain't dumb enough to do no weird shit like that," Kash said, praying he didn't attract a stalker. He slumped down lower in his seat, still studying the agents every move and how they kept their eyes on Denim's home. Her truck was still in the driveway, but of course, Kash knew she wasn't there. Dre's phone began to ring loudly in Kash's pocket. A smirk crept on his face. He now had action. It was show time.

Kash took the phone from his pocket and answered with a quick "Yo!" Dre ordered the murder of Agents Hassan and Bullock.

"Kill 'em," was all Dre said before Kash started up his car and pulled from his parking spot. Dre stayed on the other end of the receiver as Kash drove away from the scene, pressing the button on the remote he held in his hand, causing the detonator to react. A loud *beep, beep, beep* sounded, and next, a blaring *boom* echoed through the crisp night's air as the agents' car was instantly destroyed. The roof flew in the air, the doors ripped apart, the windows shattered, and the car caught on fire. Kash was too light skinned to be so damn ruthless. Nonetheless, that never stopped him from handling his business.

Lance put his fist to his lips in excitement as the agents were blown away. The entire thing was like a scene straight out of a movie.

Neither agent had a chance, never seeing their untimely death coming. Their bodies were mangled beyond recognition in the midst of it all. Kash hung up the phone as the smell of burning flesh and metal permeated Denim's block and Kash made a quick exit. There was nothing for them to stick around for. As they made their getaway down the block, Kash mused how sweet it would've been to see the agents faces as he and Lance put a bullet in both their domes; however, killing them in that manner wasn't original. Shooting was easy and too common. Nah, Kashmir wanted to do something out the ordinary. He knew the coroner would have one hell of a job trying to identify the agents' bodies.

"Yo, that shit was cold as fuck!" Lance wasn't a killer. He was a college boy who hung out with Kash while he did dumb shit. And seeing this excited him.

"Where you think the name Killer K came from? I'm a beast, G. This killing shit just comes natural."

Turning up the radio, the instrumental to Tevin Campbell's *Can We Talk?* played. He was definitely a R&B thug. As Kash made a left onto the next block, he whistled along to the tune of his favorite song.

***

Kashmir Harris, a.k.a. Kash, better known as Heaven's baby daddy, was the epitome of a real nigga. Born and raised in Chicago on the near westside, in the Abla projects, he was destined to live a life of crime. He saw and knew no other way. Kash was raised to be a hood nigga.

Being of the light skinned persuasion, as a kid, he was often mistaken as a soft individual, which in turn forced his hand on plenty occasions. At times, he found himself having to prove what he was about when it came to his gangster, which ultimately landed Kash in Cook County Juvenile Center a few times. He was a dangerous child, and nothing had changed about him as an adult. Since the age of ten, he'd been toting a pistol for protection, and he had no problems using it.

Because his home life was so dysfunctional and unstable growing up, he became a product of his environment. His home was the local trap spot. Trap niggas, drugs, weapons, and addicts were normalized in his childhood. Kashmir saw it every day. It all roamed freely in and out of his home. His mother, Doreen Harris, wasn't on drugs. Simply put, she was just lazy. She wasn't motivated to work a real nine to five. She preferred fast money. So, she allowed the men to use her place as a way to make ends meet while sitting on her ass all day. Kashmir was his mother's child. He had no real job skills, but he had a hustler's mentality. He would do just about anything to make his money.

Tall and beautiful, Kashmir's brown eyes alone were seductive. His skin was yellow, with a brownish hue, and his body build was muscular. He should've been something bigger than a criminal. But it was understandable why he chose the life of crime. He honestly never had any positive guidance growing up. He was handsome enough to be on the front cover of someone's magazine; instead, his face graced many mugshots. Still, he did what he had to do to survive. Fuck a job. That shit just wasn't for him. Hustling was in his D.N.A.

Kash never knew his father, so he grew up looking for love in the hood niggas. He had been running with Dre ever since he was a teenager. Never really having a family of his own, Dre was someone Kash looked up to. The same way Montae had taken Dre under his wing, Dre had returned the favor and done the same thing for Kash. Dre had become the big homie, something like Kash's big brother.

Although Kash was a lot older now, and trying to create a lane of his own, he still came through, like a real loyal nigga, whenever Dre called. At the drop of a dime, no questions asked, no hesitation, no matter what it was, Kash was on his way. Being a nigga who loved to kill for fun, the shit he'd done to the agents was right up his alley.

TWO

Present Day: August 1st, 2020

A diamond studded princess, Heaven was that bitch. A rich bitch with Daddy's money at her beck and call. Being the eldest daughter of Demarco Wright, Heaven didn't have to work for anything. She was twenty-one years old without any real-life skills or experiences. Besides ending up pregnant at the age of sixteen, she'd never been through any of life's woes. Her entire life, she was sheltered and protected by her father and his goons. Even her fiancé had to be approved by the family.

Heaven had a beautiful face, amazing spirit, and an even more beautiful personality. Her aura and energy were everything, but at times, it did tend to attract the wrong people.

She was short and petite. She was all of five feet and two inches tall. She resembled Lauren London with the same exact accent as NuNu, Lauren London's character in the movie ATL. She talked a little proper because she was from the suburbs and attended private schools as a kid, but she definitely had a hood demeanor, and it ran deep in her blood, thanks to her mother, Anika.

Heaven's skin was blemish free, and small dimples adorned her cheeks, whether she was smiling or scowling. Simply put, Heaven Kiana Wright was breathtaking.

She grew up in the lap of luxury, so, whatever she wanted, she got it, whether that was money, affection, or love. She'd never worked a job a day in her life; still, she owned a five-bedroom home in Decatur, Georgia and two vehicles, a gold 2020 Audi A6 and a black 2020 Hummer truck. All three things were gifts after Heaven had graduated college months prior with a bachelor's degree in business. Her family, the infamous Wright cartel, ran the entire city of Atlanta, so they had it like that. Heaven was spoiled yet humble. A brat yet her heart was pure.

Being a part of a huge drug family, she was taught how to move with precision. Heaven's life should've been perfect, still she struggled with loving a man truthfully, and she knew why. Five years prior, her heart had been left shattered to pieces by a man back in Chicago. He left her pregnant and confused with her now five-year-old, beautiful baby girl to remind her of what could've been. Her daughter, Kamelia, looked exactly like him with beautiful brown eyes, sandy brown, wavy hair, and toasted marshmallowy colored skin. The way Heaven hated Kash while she was pregnant, she never doubted for one second that her daughter would come out looking any different. In fact, little Kamelia had Kashmir's entire face and every single perfection and imperfection - from the small, dark birthmark above her left eyebrow to the beauty mark located directly underneath the left side of her lip.

Heaven let five years and her engagement to her fiancé, Derrick, deter her from pursuing any type of contact with Kash. Plus, Heaven was a little stubborn. She was upset because Kash shunned her after finding out she was only sixteen years old at the time he had gotten her pregnant, and that was only because he was twenty-one years old and couldn't believe he'd had sex with someone so young. In that moment, he felt as if he had robbed the cradle. Nonetheless, her young, teenage heart had to get over him. Now, she was a grown ass woman and still trying to get over him. But using men as a way to get Kash off her mind never worked. Thoughts of him always only went away temporarily.

Although she had only spent two nights with Kash in the past, he held her heart in the worst way, and Derrick couldn't compare. He just wasn't him. Her life was missing something, and Heaven knew she needed closure. It was time to get to the root of her own issues.

Her heart was craving a light skinned savage that the streets called Kash. From the stories Esha had told her about the work he'd been putting in in the streets lately, she knew she had to at least see him. She needed to introduce him to their daughter before it was too late. She knew Kash's lifestyle was dangerous, but that didn't stop the way she felt. He was still young and reckless, so she had to make sure Kamelia being around him was safe enough. First, she needed to relearn him. Plus, she wanted to test the waters, whatever that may be. She wanted to somehow fit into his life and get the lovin' she missed out on.

Looking up at the ceiling and rolling her eyes, fighting back tears, Heaven plopped down on her king-sized bed as she held a bawling Kamelia in her arms. Heaven didn't know what to do. Rubbing her back, ready to cry real tears herself, Heaven shushed Kamelia while rocking her back and forth. She was a punk when it came to her daughter. Heaven couldn't stand to see Kamelia cry, especially because Kamelia always cried like someone had just beaten the hell out of her. Still, tomorrow couldn't come any faster.

Nervous butterflies fluttered around in Heaven's stomach because it was almost time for her to leave for Chicago, and it was a definite guarantee she would see Kash. Thoughts of him were one thing, even the notion of building something with him, but actually being in his presence literally had Heaven feeling sick to her stomach. She didn't know if she was fully prepared for this, but Heaven was determined, and she wasn't returning to Atlanta without some type of resolution.

An hour prior, Heaven sat Kamelia down on her lap and broke the news that she was leaving tomorrow, and her papa, Sno, was on his way to pick her up. With huge, puppy dog eyes, Kamelia instantly began to break down. She fell out, crying and begging Heaven to let her go with her. Now, Kamelia's face was blush red as she clung onto Heaven around her neck, pushing her face into Heaven's shoulder as she wept inconsolably.

"Kamelia, why are you showing out right now? You are not a baby anymore."

"I am a baby," she cried.

"No, you're not. You have to be a big girl for Papa and Reign. Plus, you're going to be with Regan and DJ," she said. It wasn't that Kamelia didn't enjoy spending time with her grandparents, aunt, and uncle, she just wanted to go to Chicago with Heaven. She was spoiled as hell, and Heaven had no one to blame but herself.

"I don't like it here anymore, Mommy. I don't wanna go with Papa," she said, dry heaving at this point, trying to catch her breath. "I want to go with you." Her words trembled as her little arms gripped Heaven tighter. It took everything in Heaven not to laugh at her choice of words.

"What do you mean you don't like it here anymore?" Heaven kissed the top of Kamelia's head that was covered with sandy brown single braids and beads.

"I don't like this house. I don't like Atlanta no more. I want to move to Chicago with you in your new house."

"I'm not moving to Chicago, baby. I just have some personal things to take care of, and I will be back to get you as soon as possible."

"How long is soon as possible?" Kamelia questioned.

"I don't know, Kamelia, but Papa and Reign are going to take good care of you while I'm gone, okay?" Heaven said honestly. She didn't know how long she would be gone, but she knew for a fact that her father would take good care of her baby.

Pulling Kamelia back slightly and looking at her, she wiped her eyes. "God, you look just like him," she said, just below a whisper. These were her thoughts every time she looked at her daughter. It was like staring into the face and eyes of the man she loved to hate. Kamelia was the spitting image of Kashmir Harris.

"I don't like Papa or Reign anymore," she whined, removing her arms from around Heaven. She folded them across her chest and huffed.

"You what?" Heaven asked with furrowed brows. Her neck stiffened, and her nose flared. Kamelia had her fucked up. She repeated herself.

"I don't like Papa or Reign anymore." She rolled her eyes as fresh tears cascaded down her face. Laying back down on Heaven's shoulder, she began crying again.

"Girl, I know you fucking lying." Heaven pursed her lips together. "You better stop playing with my daddy. I'm going to tell Papa and Reign what you said when they get here," she said, giggling a little as Kamelia began to cry louder.

"Noooo!" she yelled.

Heaven and Kamelia's moment alone was interrupted when they heard a light tap at the door and a man clearing his throat. That forced Heaven to look up. She looked at Derrick and smiled slightly as he stood in the doorway with an Atlanta Hawks jersey and basketball shorts on. She could tell he'd just left the gym. Heaven couldn't help looking at him from head to toe. He was a handsome man. His neatly temple fade haircut with sponge twists and neatly trimmed beard were sexy. His mocha skin and low eye lids were alluring as well. She saw the tattoo on his neck, a full set of puckered lips with her name underneath, and on his right arm was a portrait of Kamelia when she was two years old. She had the biggest smile, the same cheesy ass grin Heaven remembered seeing on Kash's face the last time she had seen him. Even after he'd ate her pussy and fucked her over, he still had that big ass Kool-Aid mug on his face. She didn't know it at the time but having a piece of Kashmir was both a blessing and a curse. Birthing Kamelia was a blessing, but her features being an exact replica of his was a curse for her. Derrick had to be a fool, getting another man's child's face tattooed on his arm. Only if he knew how much Heaven still loved Kash.

"What's wrong with her?" he asked, his voice deep and authoritative. He stepped all the way into the bedroom. Derrick was the perfect man for a woman who would appreciate him. He was a standup guy. He loved Kamelia like she was his own daughter. She helped him become a better man. Because he didn't have any kids of his own, when he met Heaven at the age of eighteen, she helped him grow as a person. For Heaven, Derrick was determined to be a good man, lover, and an even better father to Kamelia.

Thus far, he had been a great friend and great father, and she was sure he tried to be a great lover, but she was too emotionally detached. With Derrick, it wasn't love for Heaven, but she cherished their friendship. She couldn't front. She loved the sex as well. In time, she figured lust would eventually turn into something more, plus Kamelia had taken a liking to him. The two had the perfect father and daughter relationship. It reminded her of the relationship she had with Sno. The love Derrick displayed for Kamelia warmed Heaven's heart. After Kash left her a sixteen-year-old single mother, she didn't think her baby would get the opportunity to experience a father's love. But God worked it all out. He sent Derrick in to save the day. Three years prior, he'd taken her in as his own, and ever since, he was the only man her baby girl had known. Still, Heaven was tired of living a lie.

Derrick wasn't someone permanent. She only stayed in the relationship because she didn't want to be alone and for the sake of Kamelia, but now, it was time to make herself happy. She was still young and vibrant. She still had a life to live. Her temporary move to Chicago was the first step of her journey. She couldn't help but wonder what was this universe shit her father told her about, and in all honesty, she felt like the universe was forcing her far, far away from Atlanta and to Chicago.

"You already know what's wrong with her," she said with a slight attitude, looking down at Kamelia. She closed her eyes and took in a deep breath. Derrick being in her presence right now was unwanted. She already had to deal with Kamelia's tantrum, and she was already irritated. Derrick walked over to them. He kissed Heaven's forehead, and she sucked her teeth. "Derrick." She moved her head back.

"What's with the attitude, mane?" he asked. Frowning, he gripped her chin and stared into her eyes as he tried to caress the side of her face with his thumb.

"I don't have an attitude, Derrick," she said somberly. Turning her head to the side and moving back from his grasp, she reached for her cellphone that was now vibrating on the bed. Looking at the screen, she sighed and rolled her eyes back up to Derrick.

"You sure?"

"Yes, Derrick. I'm sure," she said with a little bass in her soft voice. Expressionless, she looked back down and kissed Kamelia's forehead.

"You're lying, Heaven. But whatever. I don't want to spend tonight upset," he said, looking at her intently. "Who is that calling you?" Derrick asked, looking over at her phone. He had been suspicious about Heaven's sudden desire to go to Chicago. It was crazy to him how she continued to do shit behind his back. The entire Chicago visit wouldn't have bothered him so much; however, Heaven had been sneaking around, talking to everyone about it except for him. She'd even asked her father to find her a place to stay in Chicago, and Derrick took that as she was leaving for good to be with another man. He knew her story about her past Chicago lover. He feared she was going back to rekindle their relationship, especially since she'd been treating him like shit for the past few months.

Don't touch me… Not tonight… I'm not in the mood were all of a sudden Heaven's words of choice when it came to sex with him. Even the way she moved her face from his grasp, as if he made her skin crawl, was something new. Now, he found himself questioning her every move.

"My mama. She don't want shit though. Irritating ass." Heaven wiped Kamelia's face.

"Yeah?"

"Yep."

"Your mother has a mental illness; she can't help the shit she does," he said. "Maybe y'all should talk."

"That's all fine and dandy, but I don't have to be around her bullshit either. That shit she pulled at my daddy's house was too much for me. I personally don't have shit to say to her."

"But you can go all the way to Chicago, just to be around a nigga who left yo dumb ass..." He began but stopped after looking down at Kamelia who had stopped crying and was now looking up at him with her mouth wide open. "I'm sorry, baby," he said to Kamelia as he reached for her, but she was not having it. With her arms still wrapped around Heaven's neck, she held on for dear life.

"No!" Kamelia yelled with her head on Heaven's shoulder.

"What the fuck are you even talking about?" Heaven looked at Derrick, mugged up as she put her hand to Kamelia's ear. This conversation wasn't for her young ears. Him letting the words "dumb ass" slip from his mouth was enough for Heaven to pop him in his face because those were definitely fighting words.

Growing up, she had been a witness to her mother and father's toxic relationship. She'd seen the arguments, the fights, and she'd even been used as a pawn by Anika. So, she knew that wasn't the lifestyle she wanted to lead nor was that the type of relationship she wanted to expose her daughter to.

She had no idea where he had gotten his information from, but he had to be talking to somebody about her. He was too sure of the words he spat, and she was heated. Derrick had never talked to her in this manner. He had always handled her and her feelings with care. But this was just what she needed, an excuse to go to Chicago and do her without feeling guilty.

Although Heaven had told Derrick about her and Kash in the past, she never thought he would attempt to throw the shit back in her face all because she didn't want to have anything to do with her own mother. That wasn't his place, and it definitely wasn't any of his business. He didn't know her and Anika's history, and Heaven wasn't going to explain it. But what Derrick needed to know was he had Heaven fucked up.

"Nothing," he replied.

"It's clearly something." Standing up and situating Kamelia on her hip, she said, "You seem to know everything when it comes to my fucking life. You in this bitch advocating for Anika like you're fucking her." Heaven's voice was raised as she got in his face.

"Clearly, she is fucking you way better than I am since me being buddy buddy with her is your main gaddam concern." Her finger was pointed in his face, and her neck was on a roll as she spoke. Derrick was all of six feet tall, but that didn't stop Heaven. Her short stature didn't make her back down from an argument or fist fight with Derrick if that was what he wanted to do.

"Mommy," Kamelia whined, sitting up to look at Heaven and then Derrick. Heaven really couldn't explain it. She didn't know if the way she suddenly began to feel about Derrick was because she knew she would be reconnecting with Kash or if she genuinely didn't give a fuck about him.

"Shhhh." Heaven laid Kamelia's head down on her shoulder. She understood this moment would probably traumatize her daughter, and she knew "fucking" would possibly be a new word added to Kamelia's vocabulary, but she had to let Derrick know how she felt.

"Fucking her?" he asked with his eyebrows scrunched up. He was confused by her words. "Mane, you got issues," he said. "Come here, Kamelia. We don't need to be talking like this in front of her." This time, when he reached for Kamelia, she went to him.

She looked afraid. She had never seen Heaven so upset.

"Derrick, you know what? Fuck you. You don't even know the half. All the shit I went through as a child dealing with that crazy ass lady. So, you and what you think you know about me and Anika's relationship can go to hell," she said as she pushed past him. He looked down at Kamelia and smiled at her. Deep down inside, he was sorry for even getting Heaven started. She was a passionate person, and she stood by how she felt, especially when it came to her mother.

"Heaven, why are you this way?" He followed behind her and grabbed her arm, but she yanked away.

"Don't touch me, Derrick," she said through tears as she began to walk down the stairs.

"What's wrong with Mommy, Derrick?" Kamelia put her hands to the sides of his face, forcing his gaze away from a bawling Heaven and on to her. She loved her some Derrick. He was her father in her eyes, and she was his little princess.

"Mommy is okay. She's just emotional. The same way you are at times. Mommy doesn't want to leave you here, but she has to handle a few things. So, she is crying because she is going to miss you, princess." He kissed her cheek.

"Mommy doesn't have to cry. I'm going to be right here when she gets back," she said, looking at Derrick confusingly. "She told me I have to be a big girl for Papa and Reign, so how come she gets to cry?" Kamelia asked, frowning with her arms now wrapped around Derrick's neck. She looked at him, awaiting an answer.

"I don't know," he smiled. They stood at the top of the stairs, talking, as Heaven walked to the living room. "But she will be okay. Maybe she just needs a big hug from her favorite person."

"Who is her favorite person? Me, you, or Papa?" She wanted to know.

"Of course you are her favorite person, Kamelia."

"Yeah, I am. That was a silly question." Kamelia laughed uncontrollably as Derrick began tickling her.

Heaven smiled for Kamelia as she listened to their conversation from downstairs. Their relationship was so cute. But honestly, there was nothing left in Heaven's heart for Derrick, and she didn't know why. The man practically worshipped the ground she walked on. She didn't know what it was, but it was something about Derrick she could no longer tolerate. She wiped her tears and took a seat on her beautiful, buttery soft, peach colored, leather loveseat, looking over at the silver painted accented wall as she ran her fingers through her hair.

Ding dong! The sound of the doorbell chiming instantly ceased Derrick and Kamelia's conversation as well as Heaven's tears. She shook from her thoughts. Wiping the melancholy away, she stood up and walked to the door. She knocked imaginary wrinkles from her fitted beige maxi dress, and afterwards, she ran her fingers through her thirty-inch blonde weave. Heaven wasn't from the hood, but she looked every bit of a Bankhead off Hollywood Rd. type of chick. Her body was snatched in all the right places. Her perky breasts, plump ass, and flat stomach accentuated her curvaceous silhouette.

Ding dong! She hurriedly opened the door as she felt a hand touch the small of her back. In mid smile, Heaven rolled her eyes as Sno and Reign, along with Delilah, stood there. Sno frowned, noticing Heaven's disposition, but he didn't say anything. Instead, he did a head nod at Derrick as Derrick reciprocated the gesture, and afterwards, Sno kissed Heaven on the cheek.

"Hey, Daddy." She smiled as Sno's lips met the side of her face.

"Papa!" Kamelia jumped from Derrick's arms and clung onto Sno's leg. She was full of glee now, seeing her grandfather, as if she didn't just have a fit minutes prior.

"Hey, Kamelia," Sno said, lifting Kamelia off her feet and holding her in his arms as she began playing with the diamond encrusted, platinum cross that hung around his neck.

"Girl," Heaven said loudly. "You are so phony." She pushed Kamelia playfully.

Heaven rolled her eyes to look at Reign, but before she could say anything, Delilah said, "Dang, are you gonna let us come in or no?" With a set of AirPods in her ears, a scowl on her face, and her cellphone in her hand as she watched videos on TikTok, Delilah demanded to know. "It's too hot out here for all this 'Hey, Daddy' stuff," she fussed. "We get it. You love your father."

"What's the problem, Delilah?" Reign asked as she frowned. Sno turned slightly to look at Delilah with the same confused frown on his face.

"Naw, the question is who do you think you're talking to?" Heaven asked, and Delilah huffed, rolling her eyes. "Daddy, what's wrong with your daughter?"

"Shit, I don't know. I picked her up from your mama earlier. She's been in a bad mood all day."

"Nothing is wrong with me." She rolled her eyes again. "Now let us in."

"Delilah, watch your mouth," Sno said as she sucked her teeth. "You know I'm not with that disrespectful shit." Instantly, tears began to well in Delilah's eyes and ran down her face. All of Sno's children were spoiled and accustomed to his loving and calm demeanor, not this. He never had to raise a hand to his children, but his voice was enough to control the situation. That was all Sno had to say to put her right back in her place.

"I'm sorry," Delilah said, looking down at the ground as her tears kissed the concrete. Heaven just stepped to the side. She had nothing left to say. They all stepped inside, and Sno put Kamelia down on her feet. The men and Delilah walked away before Heaven and Reign could properly greet one another.

"Hey, Ma," she said, blowing out air. She hugged Reign.

"Hey, boo," Reign said, hugging Heaven back and then kneeling slightly to kiss Kamelia on the cheek as she still stood there. "Why are your eyes red?" she asked Heaven, and instead of her answering, Kamelia did.

"She was crying because she don't want to leave me. But I told her it's okay. I will still be here when she gets back. We need our space from each other," she lied, and Heaven laughed while shaking her head.

"For real, Kamelia?" Reign asked, laughing. Knowing how much of a mama's baby Kamelia was, she knew she was lying.

"Yes," she said, pursing her little lips together. She had to be the cutest little diva, aside from her baby girl, Regan, Reign had ever seen. "Oh yeah, and my ma said Derrick was fucking her mother, Anika." Reign's mouth fell open, and her eyes were stretched open wide.

"Kamelia!" Heaven yelled.

"What?" she dragged out, looking at Heaven as if she didn't say anything wrong.

"Don't say that anymore, Kamelia. You are not allowed to say anyone is f'ing anyone. Do you understand me?"

"Yeah," she said, folding her arms across her chest.

"Heaven, what are you gonna do with my little diva?" Reign asked, laughing.

"Kamelia, go somewhere and play. She just acted a whole fool before y'all got here. Talking about she don't like her papa and Reign no more… Ma, I almost had to fight her for saying that."

"Kamelia." Reign put her hand to her chest, as if she was heartbroken, as Kamelia smacked her lips.

"Maaaaa!" she yelled and stomped off.

"That's right, lil' lying tail, potty mouth self. I told on you."

37

N A' C O L E

THREE

Whether it was early in the morning or late at night, on most days, Kash found himself in this exact bar. Feeling like he was carrying the world on his shoulders, a burden he couldn't seem to get rid of, he was only able to think clearer when he was intoxicated. More often than not, he thought about Kamelia. He had only seen a few pictures of her because Esha didn't play when it came to Heaven, and she made sure to make Kash feel stupid about not being around his daughter. Most times, he thought about what type of father he would be to her. He knew she had a great life financially. Heaven's family had money. Still, he was curious to know what type of mother Heaven was and if Kamelia was okay emotionally. He especially wondered if Kamelia would ever forgive him when he decided to right his wrongs. He thought about his own mother and the relationship he had with her. They got along for the most part; nevertheless, she was the furthest thing from a mother in his opinion. She was more like a big homie or a big sister, who's boyfriend at the time came first. When Kash was younger, that fact bothered him. He couldn't understand what was wrong with him. Why couldn't he have a mother who loved him? However, as an adult, he understood it, and at times, he could care less.

Now, he chose to deal with his mother on his own terms, only going around her a few times a month to drop off a couple dollars to her for allowing him to use her home as a trap spot. He didn't hate Doreen; he just didn't fuck with her on a personal level. He fucked with her accordingly. It was all business when it came to her. That was why, in his heart, he knew he had to make things right with his only child and child's mother. Although he didn't know Kamelia, he loved her, and he didn't want her to resent him the same way he resented his parents.

His mother, Doreen, had given him plenty of guidance on how to make money as a kid, but she had never been there for him emotionally. When he had questions about his father, or when he had questions about life in general, Doreen couldn't help Kashmir. She was like a zombie herself, stuck in time and stuck in her ways. Doreen was trapped in her own little bubble - Kash's childhood home with a Newport dangling from her mouth and a housecoat pulled tightly around her body. She disgusted him. Still, that was his mother. They were just indifferent.

His heart was groomed to be cold. The first woman, who should've been the love of his life, was emotionally unavailable for him, and Kashmir blamed his detachment from women on her. Most times, they were just a means to an end. A quick nut or a place for him to sleep at night. He could fuck them and leave them without a second thought.

However, it wasn't that easy for him to leave Heaven pregnant with his baby. But he did what he had to do. That was a dark time in life for him. His mind was going through a lot. It was to the point that Kash was out in the streets of Chicago, living like a wild child, a mad man. In layman's terms, he was living recklessly, like a fucking savage, ready to kill a nigga just for looking at him the wrong way. He'd actually almost beat a man todeath with his bare hands the day he found out she was only sixteen. He needed something or someone to take his frustrations out on.

"Nigga, this is only $17. Where's the other 3?" he *remembered saying as he body slammed the man to the pavement and commenced to beating him unconscious. "You know not to play with my money, nigga."* Chuckling, Kash couldn't believe he had done all that over three funky ass dollars. But those were his funky ass dollars to act a fool over.

He was always taught that men didn't cry, but that night, he stayed up in tears, confused and upset. Life had him fucked up and so did this little prissy chick, Heaven Wright. He wasn't sure if he loved her or if he deeply liked her because she was pregnant with his first child, but he was going crazy mentally. His mind, he was losing it. He was so fucked up over Heaven and their situation. And he wished his mother was available for him emotionally.

That was over five years ago. Nowadays, he had pushed those thoughts about the women he felt something for to the back of his mind with the exception of Kamelia. He thought about her every day. Her ten little fingers and toes. Her beautiful face that looked identical to his. He knew he would curse her with his signature mean mug. He knew she was perfect. Kash just prayed Kamelia took after his chill side and not his barbaric ways.

"Kashmir Harris, I knew I would find you in here." Asia's loud, ghetto, obnoxious voice pierced his ears like nails to a chalkboard, making Kash cringe. She brought him back from his thoughts, and he squeezed his eyes closed tightly as he sighed. Although there was music playing through the speaker, her voice seemed to be louder.

A month prior, Kash found out Heaven would be visiting Chicago for the summer, and he had to get himself right, just in case he coincidentally bumped into her. He didn't know what he felt for her. He didn't even know if she had a man, but he knew he didn't love Asia, and if the opportunity presented itself, he would fuck with Heaven.

It had been at least two weeks now since Kash disappeared. Honestly, he was praying Asia had gotten over him by now. He figured if he was out of sight, he would be the furthest thing from her mind. It was nothing Asia had done personally. Although she was hood as hell, he liked that about her. Still, he was nervous to see the woman Heaven had become. From what he remembered, Heaven was literally the sweetest girl he'd ever met, from the taste of her body to her personality.

"You been looking for me?" he asked dryly. Fifteen minutes earlier, she came sauntering into the establishment, looking like a real-life buss down. It was twelve in the afternoon, and she looked as if she had just had a long morning out on the stroll. Her wig was honey blonde, her lips were painted red, and her make up was flawless. She had a pretty face, but her attitude was fucked up. Asia, being named after her father's birthplace, had pretty pecan brown skin and slanted eyes. She still looked every bit of Chinese or Japanese. However, her body was compliments of her African American mother and ancestors. Pretty, thick, and petite were the specific assets she used to get attention from men. With a pair of spandex booty shorts on that resembled boy shorts underwear, a top that looked like a bra, and a pair of clear, five-inch, peep toe heels, she was definitely here to demand Kash's attention. As soon as she spotted him, sitting in his usual spot, front and center at the bar with his eyes focused down, glued to a glass of clear liquor, she walked over and took a seat right next to him. He was so caught up in his thoughts that he didn't even realize she'd been sitting next to him this whole time.

"So, I have to fucking stalk you now?" She cocked her head to the side. "I haven't seen or heard from you in days. No, scratch that. It's been two weeks. Where the fuck have you been?" Her voice rose, and he looked over at her with one brow cocked upwards.

"Watch yo' tone, Asia," he said, moving his eyes from her and over to a television that hung directly in front of him. He finessed his beard.

"I'm not watching shit until you tell me where you been." She grabbed his face in between her thumb and index finger, forcing him to look at her.

Grabbing her arm and roughly yanking it away, he said, "You must be crazy. I don't owe you shit, G. Not even an explanation." With squinted eyes, he stared through her, ready to fuck her up for disrespecting him in public. Still, his voice never rose.

"I just wanted to know where you been," she said innocently. She needed answers. "You're my man, and I haven't seen or heard from you in weeks, Kashmir. Why do I have to look for you? Why do I have to beg you to want me?"

Kash smirked. He looked her up and down, and instantly, he frowned, ignoring her nice and humble tone. "Where the fuck is your clothes? You're a fucking mother. Have some dignity and respect for yourself, shorty," he said, pulling his white t-shirt over his head and handing it to her. "Put this on. Don't dress like that when you're in public with me."

Asia sucked her teeth. "You checking me about what I have on, but you still have not answered my question. What are we doing? Are we together or not? Because my nigga ain't never about to pull no disappearing act on me and then act all nonchalant about it. Who are you fucking? Which one of these nasty hoes got you acting brand new?"

Ignoring her, he looked at the bartender and yelled. "Aye, Nadia, can I get another shot?"

"Don't do that, Kash," Asia said with her lip turned up. "Don't ignore me." Looking in the direction of Nadia, Asia scowled, watching as she sauntered over towards them with a pair of black daisy dukes, the same exact shorts Asia had on, an orange and black tank top, and a pair of black, spiky, rhinestone sandals on. Nadia was thick as fuck with chunky, caramel, oily thighs, wide hips, a flat stomach, a fat ass, and small breasts. She was petite and beautiful. She was definitely a sight to see. Her curves resembled a throwback Coca-Cola bottle.

"Yeah, I gotcha, Kash." She smiled at him and then at Asia. Kash threw his first shot back and slid his glass back to her. "What can I get you?" Grabbing the glass and wiping down the countertop, she looked at Asia.

"Nothing, bitch." Asia frowned. Her eyebrows were sunken in crookedly, and her lips were turned up in a scowl as she looked at Nadia enviously. Asia didn't play about Kash, and she wasn't about to let this Nadia bitch steal her man.

Nadia's mouth was wide open as she stared back at Asia.

"Chill, Asia. I apologize about that, Nadia. She don't mean no harm… Matter of fact, I'll take three shots."

"It's cool. I know how these *hoes* are over you." Nadia emphasized hoes sarcastically, pursing her lips. "I'll be right back with your shots," she said, smirking at Asia before walking away.

"Kashmir, you just gon' sit there and let that plastic, silly built, jiggly body ass bitch call me a hoe? You lay up in my bed and in my crib every night. You know I'm not a hoe. Is she the reason you bring yo' ass up in this dusty ass bar every damn day?" She pushed his arm, and he chuckled as he hung his head in amusement. To Kash, Asia was very entertaining. Nothing about her embarrassed him because he didn't take anything about her seriously.

Asia was insecure. That much was clear. She thought everybody and their mama wanted Kash. However, she could never allow another bitch to take her man. It had only been nine months since they had been together, but Asia found herself quickly falling in lust and infatuated with Kash. He was the total package, everything Asia wanted in a man. He was a go getter, he was chill, and he didn't mind spending his time and coins on her and her three bad ass kids.

Before they got together, she was working at Captain Hooks, a small little chicken joint on the west side of Chicago, to make ends meet. Now that she had a man like Kash, she was living her best, unemployed, bougie ass life. They were living so beautifully, almost like husband and wife, with the exception of her not knowing anything personal about his life, aside from him having money. She didn't know how he made his money, and that much didn't matter to her as long as he spent it on her. Asia didn't even know Kash's home address. Often times, he would either spend the night at her house or take her to one of his spots. At times, he would fancy things up a little and take her to an Airbnb he frequented, but recently, he had been acting a little funny, wanting his own space and not coming around as much as he used to. Everything she felt was perfect in the beginning with Kash had now begun to feel a little unstable.

"Asia," he chuckled. His voice was both mellow and sexy. "Why you even here? I didn't sleep with you last night. Like you said, we haven't seen each other in weeks. How did you know where to find me?"

"Kash, you know how I found your drunk ass. You're a fucking alcoholic. Where there's an open bar, Kashmir will be there," she said with an attitude. He sat there, listening to her ramble on and on as he looked at her expressionless. He couldn't do anything but shake his head.

"You don't know shit, shorty. I've never been an alcoholic. But if you're tired of my drinking, move the fuck around. It's that simple," he said, looking at her seriously. After all the things Kash had been through in his life, he deserved a drink or two. Still, it was none of Asia's business why or when he had a drink.

She grimaced at his statement because she wasn't going anywhere. She was here to stay. "This fucking dirty ass hole in a wall. And this bitch you in here flirting with looks like her pussy stink. All I know is you better not bring me home no fucking STD."

"G, me and you definitely use condoms, and Nadia is my fuckin' cousin." With flared nostrils, he looked at her and frowned as Nadia approached the two with the three shot glasses.

"Uht." Speechless, Asia tucked her hair behind her ears and took her cellphone from her purse, pretending to occupy herself with something on the screen.

"Look at you," he laughed. "I bet you feel salty as hell. Where all that mouth at now, love?" he asked, and she sucked her teeth.

"Whatever. That bad built bitch ain't yo' cousin," she said under her breath.

"Here you go, Kash." Nadia sat the glasses down.

She opened a new bottle of Patron and poured Kash three double shots. "You look like you need more than a few single shots, lil' cuz." She laughed, and so did Kash.

"Thank you, cuz." He placed a glass in front of Asia and then Nadia.

"No problem, but you know I don't drink on the clock," Nadia giggled. With one eyebrow raised, she scooted the glass back over towards Kash. She put her hands on her hips. Her face was scowled up, and her lips dipped low, pursed together, awaiting his comeback. That was the type of relationship they always had. Being only two years apart, Kash and Nadia were close like brother and sister.

"Man, this the family business. It's not like you gon' get fired. Here, have a shot with your lil' cousin."

"I know I'm not going to get fired, cousin, but I gotta be on my shit and keep it professional, no matter who I'm serving," she said.

"Man, not using the word *shit*. That's not professional," Kash said, laughing. "Just have one shot with me. It's my birthday," he lied, chuckling.

"Boy, it ain't yo' damn birthday." She reached over and pushed his shoulder. Kash laughed, and Asia sucked her teeth.

"Damn, Kash, fuck it. You begging her and shit. The

bitch said she don't want to take a shot." Asia frowned and rolled her Asian slit eyes.

"Kash, I'm not gon' be too many of your friend's bitches." Nadia's hands were now firmly planted against the bar top as she stared through Asia.

"Asia, I'm not gon' tell you again. Cool the fuck out."

"Girl, you called me a hoe, but I can't call you a bitch?"

"No, you can't. And I didn't call you a hoe, but if the shoe fits." She cocked her head to the side.

"Yo, Nadia, Asia." He said both women's names sternly.

"What, Kash? I'm not going to say anything else to your cousin." Asia lifted her shot glass. "Can I have a lime?" she asked humbly as Nadia smirked facetiously. Nadia passed Asia a lime slice. "Cheers." She put the glass to her lips as Kash and Nadia followed suit.

"You know I don't drink this shit." Nadia made an ugly face. "But because you're my favorite little cousin, I'ma do it." They all threw the shots back, and Nadia grimaced while Kash and Asia took it like a G.

"Lightweight." Kash laughed.

"Boy, lightweight my ass. Patron is the nastiest shit

ever."

"I'm sure you've had much nastier things in that big ass mouth," Asia mumbled.

"Asia, bro, what's your problem?"

"Anyways, what's been going on? I haven't seen you in a while," Nadia asked, rolling her eyes from Asia to Kash.

"Shit. I came in here a few days last week, but Unc told me you was on vacation."

"Yep, last week me and my fiancé went to the D.R. You need to get you a Facebook, Twitter, or something."

"Nah, I don't rock with that bullshit. That's how niggas get caught slippin'," he said honestly. That blue app was a fucking trap. Asia was proof of that.

"What the hell you mean, *caught slippin'*?" Asia asked with one raised eyebrow. "You fucking someone else, Kash?"

"Man, shorty, cool out," Kash said shortly with a scowl on his face.

"Don't be showing out in front of your pretend cousin, Kashmir." Kash shook his head but didn't respond. He just looked at Nadia with pleading eyes, begging her not to respond to Asia's smart remarks.

"My daddy was filling in for me. How is Auntie Doreen?"

"She been cooling. Begging and shit. You know her usual ammo," he replied, and Asia rolled her eyes.

"Boy, stop playing with my TT. You owe her your life."

"I don't owe her shit,"

"When am I going to meet your mother, Kash?" Asia chimed in.

"What the fuck you want to meet my OG for?"

"So I can feel closer to you." Asia smirked slightly and wrapped her arm around Kash's. He looked over at her, disgusted.

"Nah." Kash was short with his response.

"Well, tell my TT I said hey the next time you go over there." As Nadia looked from Kash to Asia, she could tell he didn't like her the way she liked him.

He was lethal for quickly developing dismissive feelings when it came to relationships.

"Asia." Remembering her name from earlier, Nadia smiled, trying to rid the awkward moment.

"Kashmir is so rude, but I'm his big cousin. Our relationship is not pretend. We are very close. His mother is my father's sister," she announced.

"Nice to know. It's nice to finally meet someone in his family." Asia put on a phony smile as Kash stared through lazed eyes. This was the first person in his family she'd met, and Nadia would definitely be the last.

"Fake ass," he muttered, mockingly. "Now it's nice to meet someone in my family,"

"Kash, stop," Nadia laughed. "She didn't know. Don't be rude."

"He can't help it," Asia said shortly, unwrapping her arm from his.

"I'm not being rude. Shorty just ain't got no manners. You know I'm a laidback nigga. Ole girl just bring out the worse in me. She swear I'm fucking everything with a pussy. But this will be the last time you see her."

"Who the fuck is ole girl?"Asia asked, standing from her seat. "Nigga, you a whole fucking clown."

"Yeah, but you the mufucka out here wit'cho titties, pussy, and ass out. On me, you better watch your mouth."

"Come on, guys. Let's just take another shot," Nadia said, trying to stop a brewing altercation.

"Nah," Kash frowned. "Get the fuck on, Asia. Go home."

"Fuck you, Kashmir," she said.

"Yeah, I know." He smirked, looking her up and down as he licked his lips. "Goofy ass," he said, watching her as she walked behind his seat. He couldn't help himself. As she made her way past him, he smacked her ass. "I'ma call you later."

Asia smiled. She continued walking without saying a word. She knew she still had Kash in her clutches from that action alone.

"Kash, you is crazy. You still got these girls going wild over yo' ass." Nadia laughed, wiping off the countertop. "You are definitely your mother's child. I remember Auntie Doreen having men coming in and out the crib when we were younger."

"Yeah, that's about all she taught me. How to hustle and how to be heartless. Honestly, I don't think I know how to love. But shit, I been cooling lately. The shit I been thinking about… fucking another bitch has been the furthest thing from my mind."

"Do tell, baby cuz."

"G, I got a five-year-old daughter."

"The lies you fucking tell," Nadia said, pushing Kash's shoulder.

"Real shit, Nadia. I wouldn't play about that."

"You're telling me you have a child. A five-year-old

daughter, and I've never met her? Why am I just hearing about her? Has Auntie Doreen met her?" Nadia asked, and Kash shook his head. His chest rose slightly as he let out a breath. "No?"

"Shit, I haven't even met her." He hung his head in embarrassment. He was ashamed to admit that fact out loud.

"Kashmir Harris." She said his name scoldingly. She was disappointed in him. Knowing how he grew up, and knowing his parents weren't shit, she thought he would want more when it came to a relationship with his own children.

"I know, G. I know…"

"You kept this from me for five years? Wow."

"Man, I didn't know how to feel about the whole thing. My baby mama was only sixteen when I popped her off. I was already twenty-one. That shit fucked my head up. A nigga felt like a straight up pedophile."

"So, fuck the baby because you made a mistake? Nah, cousin, that ain't how us Harrises get down."

"Nah, it's never been fuck Kamelia. Shit, it's never been fuck Heaven. I just…" he said and looked off to the side of him, towards the door. "I haven't been able to get in contact with Heaven. Esha won't give me shorty phone number." He went to his photo app as he talked.

"Damn, cuz. Kamelia is a really pretty name though."

"Yeah, I call her Baby K." Kash turned his phone around so that the screen was facing Nadia, showing her the most recent picture Esha had sent to him of Heaven and Kamelia. "This is my daughter, Kamelia Harris, a.k.a. Baby K."

"She looks just like you. Look at all that sandy brown hair and that big ass, mischievous smile. She's beautiful, cousin… Is that her mother?"

"Yeah, that's her. Heaven Wright. Shorty bad bad."

"Where you meet her at? She look like she comes from money. She got on a $100,000 watch, and I ain't never seen a Jag in the hood before."

"Yeah, her family got a bag. They live in Atlanta. I met her out west. Esha brought her to a block party a few years back. We kicked it a couple times and shit just happened from there."

"We gotta fix this shit. Tell Lance to make Esha give you her number." Nadia frowned.

"There's no need. Lance told me Heaven will be in Chicago tomorrow. I'ma J down on her ass and see about my shorty. That's why I been tryna stay away from Asia. I got so much other shit on my plate. I don't have time to play boyfriend and step daddy."

"Step daddy? Nigga, I know like hell you ain't when you ain't even been a father to your own."

"G, don't make me feel stupider than I already feel. I know I'm wrong, and I'm man enough to admit it. I just want to fix it."

"Yeah, I know you will fix it. You're my baby cousin, and us Harrises don't play when it comes to family."

Buzz, buzz, buzz, buzz! Kash felt his cellphone buzz in his hand. He looked at the caller ID. Seeing Dre's name, he excused himself from the bar and walked to the bathroom. Kash and Dre, although they were close with Dre being Kash's mentor back in the day, they usually only talked about business.

He went inside the men's bathroom and walked over to the mirror.

"What's good, Killa?"

"Shit, G… How things been in Chicago?"

"Slow motion. Quiet ever since that lil' play I ran on them agents." Kash announced.

"That's what's up. Shit been quiet out here too. I might need you to slide on me in a few weeks. I need to introduce you to one of the lil' homies out here. Sno tryna put his son in law down with the team, move him up in the business, and I figured since you been running shit in the buildings, you two need to get acquainted," Dre said.

"That's cool. Just let me know when and where."

"I got you. What's going on with Doreen?" he asked. "She called me a few days ago, but I missed her call. Is she good?"

"Yeah, she's good. Ain't shit changed. She probably was calling to beg or some shit," Kash said, and Dre chuckled.

"Well, shit, I'm not gon' hold you up. Before we get off the phone, I need a favor from you, bro."

"What's up?"

"My partner's daughter is on her way to Chicago. I just need you to look after her while she's there."

"Maaann, I'm not no mufuckin' babysitter, G," Kash laughed.

"I know you're not, but nigga do me this favor."

"G, you need me to look after a lil shorty? How old is she? Is she pretty?"

"I mean, she's attractive. She's about twenty-one or twenty-two."

"Nah, man, I'm not gon' be able to do that," he said, chuckling and scratching the top of his head. "Asia is not gonna go for that shit. You gotta find somebody else."

"G, you the only nigga I trust. Tell Asia you on an assignment. She will understand. My mans is paying $200,000 just to watch over her for about a month. You don't have to be in her face or shit. You don't even have to interact with her. Just watch her, make sure she's straight."

"Man, I don't know about this. I got too much going on to be babysitting shorty. But that $200,000 sounds good as hell." He thought for a second. "Aight, I'll pop in on shorty, check on her, and make sure she's good."

"Aight, her plane should be landing around 1 p.m. tomorrow."

"Aight, cool. Send me her address and shit. I'll make sure she's good."

"Aight, bet!" The men hung up, and Kash made his way back to the bar. He never put two and two together. He didn't realize who Dre was asking him to watch over. He knew Heaven was from Atlanta, and her family was notorious in the streets of the A. Still the thought of him looking over her never came to mind.

He took a seat back at the bar and sat back. Ordering another drink, he put his eyes into his phone as he casually sipped his liquor. *What if old girl is Heaven?* He let the thought linger. He didn't even think to ask Dre her name or anything. "Hell naw." He chuckled before scrolling to his photo album. He looked at a picture Esha had sent him of Heaven, and he shook his head. She was beautifully put together, no longer the young, naïve, sixteen-year-old teenager whose heart and pussy he had intentionally played with. He had accomplished both things.

"Cousin," Nadia said, snapping Kash from his thoughts.

"Yeah." He looked up at Nadia and dimmed the light on his phone.

"What you over here thinking about? Your baby mama?"

"Nah. I'm tryna see where this nigga, Lance, at."

"You don't have to lie to me, cousin. I won't judge you." She pursed her lips together knowingly. "That girl got your mind gone."

"Man, I'm straight," he said.

"You may be straight, Kash, but something about you changes when you talk about Heaven and Baby K. I didn't see that same change in you when Asia was in here. Look, cousin, I know men don't like talking about their feelings or whatever, but I'm here to talk whenever you need me."

Shaking his head, Kash said, "I think about my baby often. I'ma figure this shit out… Let me call this nigga, Lance. He taking all day." It was almost as if Kash spoke Lance up as he came swaggering into the bar with his dreads pulled into a ponytail on the top of his head. His face looked scruffy as his newly grown beard sat unevenly across the bottom of his face.

"You do that, cousin. Make sure you bring my little cousin through here when you finally meet her." She smiled as Lance took a seat next to Kash. "Hey, Lance."

"What's up, Nadia?" he said as he bumped fists with Kash. "I just saw Asia outside, sitting in her car. I thought you and shorty was a done deal?" he asked.

"She followed me up here," Kash said shortly, and Lance shook his head.

"What can I get for you?" Nadia asked.

"I would say whatever Killa K been drinking." He looked over at Kash and noticed the slightly intoxicated, along with emotionally drained, look on his face and said, "But hell naw. Give me anything. Just don't give me whatever the fuck this nigga had."

"Aye, G, I been going through it," Kash replied. "Shit you wouldn't understand."

"You look like you lost your dog." Lance shook his head. "Yo, Nadia, what bitch made this nigga cry now?"

"With best friends like this goofy ass nigga, who

needs enemies? How you gon' sit here and laugh at my pain like that, bro?"

"Y'all are crazy."

"G, just give me a double shot of 1738 on the rocks. Asia got you trippin', shorty," Lance said, laughing. Nadia shook her head and laughed before walking away.

"Fuck Asia. I'ma give that bitch some dick later to situate her for a few days. But I was just telling Nadia about Baby K."

"Awe, word?"

"Yeah, she's been on my mind heavy since you told me Heaven was coming to Chicago. I watch you with your son, and I wonder what life would be like with my own child. She's older now, and I just feel like she's gonna hate me. G, I missed it all. Every single milestone. Her first word, her walking for the first time. Her first tooth, her eating her first Cheeto puff, her first day of school."

"Man, Heaven bougie ass ain't letting Baby K eat no damn Cheeto puffs. Shit, she feeding yo' shorty all rich people food. Caviar and shit." Lance laughed, trying to get Kash out of his feelings. "So, you ain't missed that *first* yet. And she have about eleven more first days of school. It's not too late."

"You a fool, G. But you feel what I'm saying. All the

things I should've been there for, I missed. It's because of Esha I even know what my daughter look like. I would've saw Baby K in public and not known who the fuck she was."

"Lies, my nigga. Baby K look exactly like you."

"Hell yeah she do," Kash chuckled. "Jo, Esha is a blessing. I appreciate the fuck outta her for keeping me up to date with my daughter."

"Yeah, Esha has a good heart," Lance said as Nadia came over with his glass of cognac on ice. "Thank you, love." He took the glass from her hand and used his thumb to softly rub hers.

"Lance, if Esha was here, would you be touching me like this?" she asked as she stared Lance in his eyes. He was an attractive man, but she was engaged, and Lance was in a committed relationship.

"You worried about the wrong shit, lil' shorty."

"I'm worried about the right shit. Lance, I don't want any beef over some dick I never had." She licked her lips.

"But do you mind beefing over some dick you can have whenever you want it?" he asked, lifting her hand and kissing it.

"Yo, y'all need me to excuse myself for a minute?" Kash asked, laughing. Lance and Nadia definitely had some type of sexual chemistry with one another, and Kash wanted no parts. The way they stared at each other and the way Nadia pretended as if she didn't want Lance touching her in front of him was all bullshit, and Kash knew it. Still, he had his own women problems to deal with. So, all he could do was shake his head.

"No. You don't have to excuse yourself, cousin. Lance, cut it out. Esha is cool. I wouldn't do that to her. So, you're gonna have to find another gullible bitch to cheat on her with." She removed her hand from his and walked away. She almost fell for him. Lance was a very charming man. Still, the hoods of Chicago were very small, and she knew that, somehow, word about her and Lance would get back to Esha and possibly even her fiancé. Nadia didn't want them problems. It was a good thing Kash was there. If he wasn't, Nadia knew she would've done something she would live to regret.

"Damn, G. I was this close to getting some love from Nadia." He shook his head and took a sip from his glass. "Look at all that ass," he said, watching as Nadia walked over to another customer.

Kash laughed. "G, leave that alone."

For the rest of the day, Kash and Lance chilled. They watched a few basketball games on TV, and in between time, Lance flirted with Nadia.

By the time the sun began to settle, both Kash and

Lance were laughing obnoxiously as they stumbled out the bar with Nadia on their heels.

"I'm good, cuz," Kash said. "I'm about to go to my bitch house and lay up," he announced.

"Nope. I'm not letting you or Lance's drunk ass drive home. So, give me your car keys." She held her hand out.

"Shit, you can have my keys," Lance slurred. "You can have this dick too. I'm going home wit' yo' thick ass anyways." He walked up on her with his bottom lip trapped in between his teeth.

"Boy!" Nadia laughed. "You got a whole woman and baby at home. Get yo' ass outta here."

"So."

"So, my ass. Esha is cool peeps. Plus, I'm engaged. I'm about to drop yo ass off at home, and you too, Kashmir."

"Nah, just drop me off at my Ching Chong bitch crib."

"Kash, shut yo' drunk ass up. What the hell is a Ching Chong bitch?" She laughed.

"You know." Kash put his fingers to the sides of his eyes, making them low and slanted. "Chung Li. Them bitches that be in the nail shop gluing them big ass lashes on y'all eyes." He and Lance laughed hard as hell.

"Kashmir, just shut up. Come on," she said as she crossed the street and began walking towards her car.

"G, your cousin… Shorty is sluggin'," Lance whispered, tapping Kash's shoulder as he watched her ass bounce up and down. "Hold up, Miss Judy. That's a big ass booty, shorty." Lance flirted, running up behind her and grabbing her waist.

Beep, beep, beep! The loud horn forced the three to turn their heads in its direction. When Kash saw Asia's car, he stopped walking.

"This crazy bitch been sitting out here all this time?" He shook his head.

"Kash!" Asia yelled out the window.

"There goes Miss Chung Li," Nadia laughed.

"Man, go handle that. Don't worry, bro. I'ma handle cousin Nadia tonight and make sure she get home safely." He looked at her, smiling as he entered her space again in the middle of the street.

"Lance, back the fuck up," she said. "Don't make me call your baby mama on you," she threatened.

"Damn, love, you gon' snitch on a nigga?" he asked.

"Kash!" Asia yelled again and hit the horn.

"She gon' beat you the fuck up if you keep playing." Lance stopped flirting with Nadia long enough to say.

"Shorty ass be tweakin'." Kash sighed.

"You better go ahead, Kash. I'm not going to help you when she start swinging on yo' ass. You and Lance wanna be playboys so bad and don't even know how to play the game."

"Hold up, shorty. I ain't never been a playboy. I'm the good guy. You tryna find out?"

"Hell naw!" she said loudly. Her voice echoed down the block.

"Kashmir!" Asia said, laying on the horn. *BEEEEEEEPPPP!*

"Hold the fuck on, goofy ass girl!" he yelled back.
"Y'all ass a fool, but I'ma catch up with y'all later. Lance, don't forget we got a 10:30a.m. basketball game. I'ma meet up with you at your OG crib around 9. Don't be late, G. After that, I gotta go babysit."

"Babysit? Nigga, what?"

"Dre got some shorty coming up here. He need me to check in on her."

"Dre, how that nigga doing?"

"He straight. Bro down in the A doing his thing. But

look, let me gon' head and get outta here before I have to choke her ass. Y'all be good."

"Alright, cousin. Love you." Nadia hugged Kash.

"Bring yo' thick ass on, G." Lance licked his lips. "Nadia about to have me up all night," he yelled at Kash as he walked away, chuckling.

"Boy! Boo. I'm about to drop your ass off at your home." Nadia sucked her teeth and proceeded to walk off. "See you, cousin."

FOUR

After spending about an hour chit-chatting with Reign, Heaven was in a disarray of emotions as she went upstairs to retrieve the things Kamelia would need for the next few weeks. She took a seat on the rocking chair she had spent plenty of nights rocking Kamelia to sleep when she was a baby. She set her phone down on her lap and put it on silent as she let out a breath, exhaling her emotions. Now that she was alone, she had time to herself and her thoughts.

Derrick's words had really gotten to her, more than she wanted to admit. She was full of mixed emotions, feeling as if maybe he was right. Maybe she really was a dummy for wanting to explore anything with Kash. Yeah, he was the man who helped her create life, but that was where their story ended. He never tried to pursue anything further than that. Still, he deserved to know his daughter, and his daughter deserved to know him. And as far as her mother went, fuck what Derrick thought he knew about her and Anika's relationship. She didn't owe her shit. Her mother was no one important to her. Anika was nutty as hell, and Heaven had every right to maintain her peace, and she knew Anika was detrimental to disturbing that.

She put her face into her hands and cried. She was so confused about life. At the age of twenty-one, she thought she would have everything figured out by now, but that was a whole lie. Sno breathed positivity into her every single day, even as an adult, but she had no clue what she really wanted out of life. However, she knew she wanted love and happiness that didn't come from her father or relatives. She knew she couldn't handpick her relatives, but handpicking a family was a whole other story.

Her relationship with her father, Sno, was perfect, and her relationship with her daughter, Kamelia, was more than she could pray for, considering her relationship with her own mother. Her relationship with her grandparents was the best, and Heaven and her siblings relationship was beautiful. Even her relationship with her stepmother was great. Heaven couldn't lie; the friendship she had with Derrick was even immense, but it was those forced relationships that brought her to tears, and anything with Anika was forced.

The relationship she had with her mother was eating at her. She understood some children didn't get along with their parents, and most times, it stemmed from strictness. However, in the past, Heaven could only wish Anika was strict with her, or at least pretended like she gave a fuck about her instead of using her for her own selfish agendas. She never wanted to be that type of mother or that type of woman. Heaven never wanted to be so crazy over a nigga that she compromised her child's happiness.

As she removed her face from her hands and looked up at Kamelia's packed suitcases, she wondered if what she was doing was from genuine intentions. Her mind wondered if she was doing the right thing. Was she really doing this for her daughter and not her own selfish agenda? She needed someone to talk her out of this trip to Chicago but who? She didn't have anyone to make this shit make sense. Her mind was acting bipolar as fuck. One minute she heard, "Bitch, you better not!" and seconds later, her mind told her she and Kamelia deserved Kash.

Interrupting her thoughts, she looked down at her lit up, vibrating phone. Anika's name showed up on the screen and Heaven took a deep breath. She couldn't ignore her mother forever, and since she was already in an emotional state, she figured right now would be the best time to hash things out with her. Heaven had never shared her feelings with Anika while they were in their rawest form. She deserved these emotions. She needed to feel the hurt that she harbored daily. Wiping her eyes and then her nose, she answered.

"Hello." Heaven cleared her throat and sat up slightly so that her feet were planted to the floor, and the rocking chair was no longer rocking.

"Hey, Heaven." Anika's voice was full of anguish as well. Heaven could tell she was crying from the cracked voice and sniffled nose. Still, she wasn't going to let Anika's tears deter her from expressing how she felt.

"What's wrong with you?" Heaven's tone came off cold and irritated. She'd never seen or heard Anika cry besides the day of Sno and Reign's wedding when she made a complete ass of herself. She wasn't in the mood to deal with anyone's feelings but her own. "And what did you do to my sister?"

"I didn't do anything to Delilah. You know how you Wright girls are. She's just spoiled as fuck, just like you… And don't be questioning my child either. She will come around soon. She's just a little confused right now."

"Us Wright girls have a father who gives a damn about us. That's the one thing you did get right," Heaven mumbled.

"I didn't catch that. What was that little smart shit you just said, Heaven?"

Heaven sucked her teeth. "Nothing," she lied. "What is Delilah confused about?"

Exhaling loudly, Anika said, "Heaven, I need to tell you something."

"I'm listening." She lifted her hand and looked at

her pastel pink, white, and silver polished, rhinestone nails. Heaven was very uninterested in what Anika had to say, but out of the little respect she had for her, she listened.

"I don't care what you think or feel about me. I know that bitch, Reign, and your father has put so much bullshit about me in your head, but at the end of the day, I pushed you outta my pussy. You're my child."

Heaven laughed. "Anika, ain't nobody told me shit about you. Remember I lived with you most of my life. I know you and what you are capable of. I remember all the fucked-up shit you put me through. I know I'm your child. That much is obvious. I am also my father's child. He's one of the most important people in my life. Just tell me what you called me for," Heaven said, and Anika sucked her teeth. She was saying all these things to purposely hurt her mother's feelings.

"You know what? Fuck it. I don't even know why the fuck I called you. You always loved Demarco more than you loved me," Anika cried. "You always chose him over me. Even after that bitch, Reign, disrespected me and swung on me, you chose their side."

"The same way you always chose these niggas over me and my sister. When it came to you and Reign fighting, Anika, you started that entire altercation..." She paused, took a breath, and asked, "Did you take your medication today?" Her facial expression was now a scowl.

"Heaven, you're my child, but I'm starting to dislike you."

"You're starting to dislike me? Wow, Anika Davidson."

"You know what, Heaven Wright? Fuck you," Anika said before hanging up. Hearing the phone disconnect in her ear, Heaven removed it and looked at the screen. She thought about how she had just snapped on Derrick earlier and how she sounded exactly like Anika in that moment.

"Lawd." She closed her eyes and shook her head. "I love you too, Ma," she said to herself.

"Heaven." Almost instantly, she heard a soft voice that was also in tears say her name. Looking towards the door, she saw Delilah, who had been standing in the hallway the entire time.

"What's wrong, baby? Come here." Heaven held her arms out as Delilah walked over to her. She stood up as Delilah reached her. Pulling her in by her arms, Heaven hugged her tightly. Earlier, when she saw her little sister, she knew something was wrong. It was written all over Delilah's face. She saw all the pain, and of course, she could relate. She even heard it in Delilah's tone, but her attitude was something Heaven had never seen. She wanted to grab her sister and hug her right then and there because Delilah was who

Heaven used to be twelve years ago when she was only nine years old and mixed up in her mother's BS. "Talk to me," Heaven said.

"I can't,"

"Why not? I'm your big sister. You can tell me anything," Heaven said as she held Delilah at arms length.

"Mama told me not to. She said it will ruin our family."

"Delilah, nothing could ever ruin us as a family. I just want to make sure you're okay." As Heaven said that, Delilah wrapped her arms back around Heaven.

"Mama took me to see some man in jail."

"What?" Heaven pulled back from Delilah again and gripped her chin, forcing her to look up at her.

"Anika did what?"

"Shhh," Delilah said. "Keep your voice down, Heaven. Mama told me not to tell anyone." She removed her face from her hand. Wrapping her arms back around Heaven, she cried into her chest. Frowning, Heaven looked down at the top of Delilah's head. She was so confused. As soon as Delilah told her this information, she wanted to run to Sno. In her heart, she was still daddy's little girl. She didn't know how to fix Delilah's problem, but Heaven knew their father would make everything better.

"Wait, Delilah. You can't just tell me some stuff like that and ask me to keep quiet about it." Heaven unwrapped Delilah's arms. She pulled her to the rocking chair and helped her sit down. Kneeling before her, she looked at Delilah in her red, teary eyes. "You know you're my heart, right?"

"Yes." She nodded her head before hanging it and looking into her fidgety hands.

"Whatever you tell me about what happened at the prison, I won't say anything unless you give me the okay to do so. Regardless of anything, you are my little sister. You're my little mini me, and I love you."

"Okay," she said, still looking down as she spoke as if she was ashamed or embarrassed. "I love you too."

"What happened?"

"Mama has been taking me to see some man named Bully. He is so ugly, Heaven."

"Bully? What type of name is that?"

"I don't know. Mama said his real name is Donterio Brown."

"I don't like his name. Bully is a better name."

"Heaven, who cares about his name? Mama is telling me this weird looking guy is my father."

"You're right, sister. I'm sorry."

"He just kept smiling at me, asking me things about school and my life. He looked sick too. He is so skinny and disgusting looking." Delilah sniffled, wiping her nose. "Mama told me to call him Daddy, but I said no. That man is not my dad. My daddy's name is Demarco."

"Right," Heaven said, frowning.

"When I refused, she yelled at me."

"Are you sure, Delilah?" Heaven asked, knowing Delilah was probably being honest. Nonetheless, kids at her age had a huge imagination.

"Yes, I'm sure. I'm not a baby, Heaven. I'm almost ten years old. That wasn't the first time I went there with her. But this was the first time she made me talk to him. She made me tell him I love him before we left, and on our way home, she told me he is my real daddy."

"Delilah, I am so sorry."

"Daddy isn't my daddy, and you're not my sister," she said and looked back up at Heaven with her bottom lip poked out as she began to cry aloud.

"Delilah," Heaven frowned. "What do you mean Daddy isn't your daddy and I'm not your sister?" As soon as she said that, she heard a gasp at the threshold of the door.

"Heaven, Delilah, what is going on?" Reign asked, stepping into the room with her hand to her mouth.

"Heaven!" Delilah yelled, looking at her with furrowed brows. She wiped her eyes and stood, almost knocking Heaven over. "You said you wouldn't say anything." She ran from the room.

"I didn't…" Heaven yelled as Delilah ran down the stairs. Standing up, Heaven wiped at her face. "Oh my God. I know you heard our conversation. This is some bullshit."

"Yes, I heard your conversation. But I'm confused as hell," Reign said with a slight chuckle. She unconsciously rubbed her small baby bump, and Heaven noticed.

"I can't believe Anika is telling my sister that bullshit. It's like she wants me and Delilah to be just as fucked up in the head as she is."

"I'm just at a loss of words right now."

"Wait, is Daddy not my daddy?" She bucked her eyes. "Literally, she just called me crying right before I talked to Delilah. Maybe she was calling to tell me the same thing."

"Don't be crazy, Heaven. Demarco is your father. You look just like him." Reign wrapped Heaven up in an embrace. "And Delilah is his daughter too," she said, not really too sure. Delilah had none of Sno's features. It was a fact that Delilah looked exactly like Anika. Still, Reign knew looks weren't a paternity test.

"Delilah isn't my father's daughter, Ma. I've known this for years, but I never had proof. I heard my mama say it one day to her friends. She always snuck men in and out the house."

"Damn." Reign kissed the top of Heaven's head.

"My dad is going to lose it when he finds out. I just hope he doesn't do anything crazy."

"He won't. Let me deal with him. For now, let's keep this between us. I will figure out a way to tell your father. I will also talk to Delilah."

"Okay, Ma. I love you so much, Reign."

"I love you too, boo. Let me get a couple of Kamelia's bags. Your father is about ready to go."

"Uhh, no." Heaven pulled away from Reign, giggling. "You are not lifting no bags around me. Don't think I didn't notice that belly." Heaven rubbed Reign's stomach. It was small but firm, and her navel was beginning to protrude slightly.

"Let's keep this between us too." Reign smiled.

"Mr. Wright doesn't know?"

"Nope, not yet, but I plan to tell him soon. I'm only ten weeks. Your father is going to have me on bedrest, and I'm not ready for that yet."

"You are huge to be only eight weeks."

"I know. It's twins again."

"Oh my God! I'm so happy for you, Ma."

"Yeah, yeah. That's why you gotta hurry up and find your baby daddy so you can come back home and help me with these babies." She laughed.

"I got you. As soon as I figure my stuff out, I will be back home. I hope it's two boys this time to even us out."

"Yeah, me too, but if not, we will still be happy."

Hearing Sno and Derrick's voices approaching Kamelia's bedroom, Heaven and Reign ceased their conversation. They both looked at the door as the men walked in.

"When Heaven comes back from Chicago, we're gonna start planning our wedding." Heaven frowned as Derrick walked up to her. She had no plans on marrying him, especially not so soon. She was still trying to figure her own shit out. He lifted her chin and kissed the tip of her nose, and she grimaced.

"Oh wow. I can't wait," Reign said, smiling, but Sno's expression was confused as he stood behind

Reign with an arm wrapped around her waist. He knew Heaven didn't want to marry Derrick. Plus, he had just given her everything she needed to stay in Chicago permanently if things for her went as planned.

Heaven sighed as Derrick wrapped his arm around her shoulders.

"We definitely want to hire your friend, Jayla, for everything in regards to the wedding," he said, lifting Heaven's hand and kissing her ring. Heaven was silent. She just stood there with a fake smile on her face.

"Sounds like a plan."

"Anywho, these are all Kamelia's bags. You guys have fun carrying them downstairs." Heaven removed herself from Derrick's arm.

"Shit, you better tell Kamelia to come up here and get her own bags," Sno joked as he and Derrick began removing her bags from the room.

It took two trips from Kamelia's bedroom to Sno's car, and they were all ready to leave.

Lifting Kamelia up from the ground, Heaven kissed her all over her little face. "Mama's baby, I'm going to be back home soon to get you, okay?"

"Yes, Mommy," Kamelia said, whining.

"Make sure you FaceTime me every day, okay?"

"Okay," Kamelia said, rubbing the side of Heaven's face. Heaven smiled at her and kissed her one last time before walking her family outside. She looked at Delilah and saw how sad she looked. Even after exposing the truth to Heaven, she looked no where near relieved.

"I love you, Kamelia."

"I love you too, Mommy." She put her down on the ground.

"Delilah, come and give me a hug," she said as Delilah walked towards the car with her head down. She stopped in her tracks and walked over to Heaven.

"What's wrong, Delilah?" Sno asked, noticing how distant she was.

"Nothing." Both Reign and Heaven answered for her. Heaven wrapped her arms around Delilah and hugged her.

"I love you, baby. Everything is going to be okay," Heaven whispered.

"Yes," Delilah replied before getting into the car. Now it was time for Heaven to turn the page to the next chapter in the book called her life.

***

His fine ass… Heaven's thoughts drifted, and her inner cheek became entangled in between her top and bottom canine teeth as Derrick entered the bedroom with a towel wrapped around his waist. He was shirtless, and his skin glistened with oil that made his tatted body look immaculately delicious. With two glasses in his hands filled with Remy 1738, and a sexy scowl on his face, it was clear what he had in mind. Heaven knew Derrick wanted to fuck her before she left for Chicago. In all honesty, she wanted to fuck him too, but after the long and emotional day Heaven had, she just wanted to sleep the entire night away.

So, she pretended as if he wasn't even there. The sex between them had always been good, but she knew a piece of goodbye or see you later dick would be even better. Still, she was drained. I mean, if I just lay here and let him take control, I won't have to do much but flex my pussy muscles, she thought as she laid out in bed with her head propped up on a few pillows. With only a pair of panties on, she was comfy underneath the covers. Her thirty-inch, lace front, sewed down wig was wrapped and tied down with a silk scarf, and her eyes were in her phone observantly watching videos on Facebook.

But discreetly, she watched him as he dimmed the lights. She took the phone from her vision and placed it underneath her nose. She followed him with her eyes as he walked over to the bed and took a seat next to her. He exhaled, handed her one of the glasses he held in his hand, and set the other one down on the nightstand. Heaven wasted no time gulping down the liquor.

"Thank you," she said after drinking it all down. Passing her glass to him, he set it down next to his.

Heaven laid there, watching him the entire time through tipsy eyes. Derrick quickly popped a half of pill into his mouth and held it on the tip of his tongue as he reached for his glass and drank the 1738 down. Heaven smiled. She knew the sex was about to be so fucking good. He was about to fuck her like he didn't want to lose her, and she was ready to take it like a champ. As he set the glass back down, she set her phone down, preparing herself to go at it. He turned to the side, and with one swift motion, Derrick threw the covers from Heaven's body, startling her. She screamed, and he laughed. He had never gotten physical with her, but this caught her off guard. He stood up, and with her legs wide open, he pulled her to him.

"What are you doing?" she asked. "I'm still mad at you." No lie, she was still a little salty about his comment from earlier. They always had small disagreements, but Heaven didn't think he would bring up her past.

"I'm sorry. Shit just been crazy between us, but I would never want you to feel like I don't love you."

"It's not about if you love me or not, Derr..." she began, but Derrick put a finger to her lips, shushing her.

"Let me finish," he said. "I don't want you to think I'm not empathetic to the things you've been through in your past, and I don't want you to leave here upset," he sighed. "Heaven, I don't want to lose you."

"I don't need you to empathize with my past. I'm no one's victim, Derrick. I chose this life. Having a baby didn't hinder me. Fuck a daddy, you know I'm a damn good mother," she said.

"I know. You're a great mother, a great woman."

"Sure, I am. I'm just dumb, right?" With a crooked smirk on her face, she wrapped her legs around him, squeezing him with her thighs.

"Nah, I was just pissed earlier. I love you, mane."

"Mmhm, I guess my dumb ass accepts your apology," she said sarcastically, laughing.

"Just be quiet, mane," he said, licking his lips.

"Why?"

"Because I said so." Pulling open the nightstand's drawer with one hand and massaging her thigh with the other, he looked down at her seductively. His facial expression was sexually motivated. His eyes were low, and his smile was crooked as he licked his lips.

"What's in there?" she asked, staring at him with

equally seductive eyes. He grabbed a bottle of massage oil from inside and showed it to her. "Oh okay. After a long, stressful day, I need this massage." She closed her eyes as Derrick poured the liquid on one thigh and then the other.

"I know exactly what you need, shawty. Just lay yo' ass back and let me help you relax." He sat the bottle down and rubbed the oil on her thighs, and she moaned while arching her back. She had nothing to say. The way his fingertips dug into her skin; she was left speechless. Her body tingled, specifically her pussy. She closed her eyes, feeling as if she would have an orgasm at any moment. This was what she meant about him being a great man. He catered to her needs. He apologized to her, even when he wasn't wrong, and somehow, he always knew what to do to make her feel appreciated. Still, she needed more than this. Euphoria felt great, but when the bliss was over, she was back to feeling as if her heart was missing something. But she was going to take this massage, pampering, and dick all night long.

Derrick watched Heaven's beautiful face. Her mouth was open slightly, which made her cheeks cave in on both sides, displaying her dimples. Lifting her left leg, he moved down to her calf and then to her foot that was now propped up on his shoulder. Rubbing and caressing her, he made sure she didn't leave Atlanta without him on her mind.

"Derrick," she cried, panting through labored

breaths. "That's enough. Take your towel off." She winked at him.

"I can't do a half job." He smiled at her as he began to rub her right leg. Derrick was so chocolate and so handsome, half naked and all. Heaven stared at him directly in his face, his brown eyes especially.

"It's fine, Derrick," Heaven said, trying to pull at his towel. It was unusual for her to even feel anything sexual when it came to him. Most times when she made love to him, she did it out of obligation.

He dropped her leg and reached over atop the nightstand, retrieving the other half of his pill. He put it in his mouth, untied the towel from around his waist, and leaned down on top of Heaven, coming face to face with her. She wrapped her legs and arms around him, holding on to the back of his head. Derrick began to kiss Heaven's lips passionately, causing her mouth to open slightly as he fed her the ecstasy pill with his tongue. Without a second thought, she swallowed it. These pills were like candy to her, and she loved the way they made her feel.

"You ready?" he asked in a low, sexy tone. His pill and liquor had already kicked in, and he was ready to make love to her all night.

"Of course," she replied as she took his bottom lip and tongue back into her mouth. She was just as ready. Her pill hadn't taken its full effect just yet; however, her body began to think for itself. Suddenly, her vagina had a mind of its own.

Before meeting Derrick, Heaven was on the straight and narrow. She had never touched a drug; she'd never even thought about it. Not even weed. In the past, while she was in the care of her mother, she only dibbled and dabbled in small recreational things like liquor and sex, but after becoming pregnant with Kamelia and moving in with her father permanently, she found herself focusing on more important things. School and the health of herself and her baby became her number one priority. Not to mention, she isolated herself from her friends, so she had no one persuading her judgement. It wasn't until she began a relationship with Derrick that she found herself becoming a whole new person.

It all began with Derrick being something like Heaven and Kamelia's bodyguard. He knew his job description, and he did his job well, but if he had to be with her every single day, he knew that one day soon they would take things further than employee and employer. He was new to all of this. The whole thought of catering to a woman was brand new to him. Picking up bags and shit would've been cool if he was dicking her down too. But he was hired to do a job. His duty was to protect Heaven and Kamelia.

No matter if it was just a quick store run, Derrick was either right on the side of her, in the passenger seat, or in the driver's seat. Still, he never tried anything slick with her. Sno had made it very clear that he was here to protect Heaven, and that was it. Derrick didn't want to overstep his boundaries.

Nonetheless, the more they hung around each other, the more they began to feel one another. It was crazy to him. Just being around her, conversing with her, being polite to her, being professional with her, and the entire time he dreamed about being with her intimately.

It didn't take long before the two found themselves together, in a relationship. For the past couple years, he had been one of the men who watched over her. To him, they already had some type of connection considering the many personal conversations they had while they were alone.

"Let me get that bag for you, shawty," Derrick said, taking a bag full of clothes from Heaven's hand that she'd just picked up from the backseat. Heaven, along with Derrick and Kamelia, had just spent the past few hours inside Neiman Marcus.

"Thank you, Derrick," she said, smiling. Reaching back inside the car, she unbuckled Kamelia from her car seat and picked her up.

"No problem." Standing back with his hand on the top of the passenger's door, Derrick followed Heaven with his eyes as she placed Kamelia on her hip.

"What?" she asked, blushing. Heaven would be

lying if she said she didn't like him, especially when he looked at her with admiration. She knew she had to be a whole snack to him, and she was ready to let him eat her up.

"Nothing, Miss Heaven."

"Are you sure?" She smirked while frowning.

"Nah, I have a few questions, but we can't talk about it around little baby ears," he said.

"Mmm." She turned around and began walking towards the front door of her father's home. Slamming the car door and setting the alarm, Derrick took a look around the neighborhood, watching their surroundings before jogging to catch up with Heaven. Reaching her, he began to walk a couple paces behind her and Kamelia. Kamelia was clearly tired as she stared at Derrick blankly. She put her index and middle fingers into her mouth, sucking them as she played with Heaven's long weave with her other hand. As she put her chin into Heaven's shoulder, Derrick smirked. He waved his hand at her and crossed his eyes while scrunching his lips up as if something smelled foul. Kamelia laughed out loud.

"What's so funny?" Heaven asked, looking over her shoulder and back at Derrick. He quickly straightened up his face and licked his lips, smirking.

"Dewick making funny faces," Kamelia laughed. At the time, she was only two years old and unable to properly pronounce 'R' words.

Stopping in her tracks and turning to look at him, Heaven smirked. "Derrick, what type of funny faces were you making?"

"Kamelia trippin'. I wasn't making no damn..."

"Uhm, Derrick, watch your mouth," Heaven said, placing her hand to Kamelia's ear as Derrick covered his mouth.

"My bad," he chuckled, removing his hand and licking his lips.

"Dewick is lying, Mommy. Him face was like this," she said, sitting up and screwing her face up to imitate his.

"Oh my God, Kamelia." Both Heaven and Derrick laughed.

"My face ain't look shit..." Heaven cut her eyes at him, squinting. "I mean, my face didn't look nothing like that."

"You have such a potty mouth, Mr. Derrick. But instead of making silly faces, can you make sure we are safe?" Her left eyebrow rose.

"Yes, ma'am, Miss Heaven Wright. I gotcha." Heaven turned and continued walking as Derrick followed closely behind her. Every so often, he would take a glimpse at her ass before looking over his shoulder, making sure they were still safe. Knowing he could never be with her the way he really wanted to, he couldn't help but to look. "Damn," he said in a hushed tone, rubbing his chin and licking his bottom lip.

"Are you looking at me or our surroundings?" Heaven asked, turning around and catching Derrick staring at her. He chuckled.

"Both." Derrick instantly made Heaven blush.

"What do you think about us going on a date tonight?" He walked up on her. He was tired of beating around the bush. Even though he knew he was overstepping his boundaries when it came to his employment, he couldn't help but to try his luck.

"Uhm," Heaven said, situating Kamelia on her left hip. "I don't think my father will be okay with that."

"He doesn't have to know. I'll just tell him I'm driving you to a party or some shit… I mean…" he chuckled, rubbing his chin. "I can make up something believable to tell him."

"Derrick, I am eighteen years old, too grown to be lying to my father, just to go out on a date," she said, smiling. He bit down on his bottom lip.

"You don't need his approval then."

"You work for us, Derrick. Sometimes it's best not to mix business with pleasure." The entire time she talked, he stared at her lips. She turned around and continued to walk. Kamelia smiled at Derrick, and he stuck his tongue out.

"Who said anything about me pleasuring you?" he asked, grabbing Heaven's arm and turning her around.

Her eyes met his, and she took a deep breath. Something about his touch was electric. She felt the sexual tension between herself and Derrick but knew she couldn't let things get to that extent. Fanning herself, she pursed her lips together.

"I tell you what. If you're comfortable going to my father as a man and asking him to take me out on a date, then I will consider it."

"Damn, shawty, you acting like I'm asking for your hand in marriage."

"I mean, take it or leave it." She forced Kamelia's head down on her shoulder before turning and walking away once again, leaving Derrick standing there, thinking. She reached the front door, twisted the doorknob, and walked inside.

Say less, he thought to himself before walking up to the front door as well.

Needless to say, he went to Sno as a man, and Sno approved. Derrick had been doing such a good job of taking care of Heaven and Kamelia, and he knew if things turned into a relationship, his daughter and granddaughter would be Derrick's number one priority. What Sno didn't know was that Derrick had introduced Heaven to a fucked-up habit. From that very first night they kicked it, she became accustomed to popping pills and sex. Now, three years later, Heaven had to be intoxicated in order to enjoy sex with Derrick. It wasn't that the sex was bad, she just no longer had a sexual attraction to him. Still, this was their last night together for a while.

As he trailed kisses from her lips to her chin, Heaven gripped him with her nails. Her eyes rolled to the back, and she gasped as he began tongue kissing her neck. Now that the pill had taken its full effect, Heaven was ready for him to fuck her. Heavy breathing, soft moans, and loud kisses echoed throughout the spacious bedroom as Derrick made his way in between Heaven's breasts. Taking his time, he made his way down to her stomach with lingering licks, making sure he didn't miss an inch of her skin.

"Derrick," she whined, sucking her teeth and rolling her eyes. At this point, her vagina was soaking wet, so she knew his dick had to be rock hard. She wasn't into the lovemaking antics and everything that came along with it. All that slow stroking and soft kisses wasn't something she wanted from him.

"What's wrong?" he asked, putting his kissing and licking on pause to look up at her.

"I'm getting sleepy," she sighed. "I'm not in the

mood for this extra shit. Just get in this pussy and fuck me to sleep," she said. At this point, she could care less how her words made Derrick feel. Still, she was a little careful with her words because she didn't want to hurt his feelings too bad. These pills ain't even working no more. This boring ass shit, she thought.

"You're getting sleepy?"

"Yes, I been up all day, packing Kamelia's things."

"So, what I'm doing to you is boring? Me making love to you don't feel good?" he asked, and she sighed. Heaven sucked her teeth.

"It's not that deep, Derrick. Don't sit here and hurt your own feelings."

"Damn, mane, you always fucking up the mood… What the hell that's supposed to mean, don't hurt my own feelings?"

"Nothing, Derrick. Are we fucking tonight or not? I have an early morning flight to catch. I need to go to bed." She was clearly annoyed. Still, she didn't mean to say what she said in the tone she did, but it was too late to take it back.The entire time they talked, he was still on top of her. So, he got up, feeling a little disrespected.

"Damn, Heaven. Straight like that, huh?"

"Straight like that."

"I'm not gon' see you for a minute, shawty. I don't like the way you're carrying me right now. Like I'm a nigga that just come through and give you some dick every now and again. I'm your fucking fiancé. I sleep next to you every single night. It ain't about to be no mufuckin' five-dollar Uber rides home after we're done making love, shawty. So, check yo' fucking mouth."

"Derrick, please. You know what the fuck I meant." Heaven sat up and climbed from the bed. She sucked her teeth and rolled her eyes, standing directly in front of him.

"You talk all that bullshit about your moms, but you're exactly like her. Mane, I cannot make this shit up. You're so fucking toxic." Derrick wasn't usually this soft. His murderous past was why Sno entrusted him to protect his daughter and granddaughter in the first place. But for Heaven, he let his guards down. He allowed her to talk to him crazy, and he allowed her to take advantage of his giving heart.

"Don't start with me. Toxic? Maybe. Me being exactly like Anika? You have me all the way fucked up. If I was anything like her, I wouldn't give a damn about you or your feelings."

"You don't give a damn about my feelings, Heaven."

"Derrick, fuck you. Oh, my bad. You couldn't even

do that right," she said, folding her arms across her chest as she stepped back slightly. "Now I don't give a damn about your feelings. Boring ass. Bitches my age like to be flipped and shit. Not slobbered on. That shit is nasty." Today had been a rollercoaster of emotions for Heaven. Usually, she either hated him or she loved on him. Every day it was either or, but today, for some reason, it was a mixture of both. "If you're gonna eat my pussy, then get your ass down there and do it instead of slobbing on me."

Derrick chuckled silently and stood. "It's funny how none of the other bitches I've fucked with complained," he said in an attempt to piss her off.

"Tuh, they must be some old bitches."

"Heaven, why are you so fuckin' combative and condescending? Sometimes I hate I even started fucking wit' you."

"Combative? Condescending?" Her tone was sarcastic. She laughed. "You hate you started fucking with me, Derrick? Huh?" she asked, walking into his face.

"You act like a little ass girl, mane."

"So, you spoil me every fucking day and then complain when I act this way? You created this attitude."

"I didn't create shit. You created that bullshit. What

grown ass woman complain about her man showing her love and attention? Don't worry, shawty. I wasn't going to leave no marks on you." He frowned.

"What are you trying to insinuate? Because who said anything about you leaving marks on me or that even being a problem?"

"I'm not insinuating shit. You sitting here, talking about how girls your age don't like this and don't like that, like we ain't been fucking the same exact way for years," he yelled. "I been fucking before I met you. I know how to please a woman."

"I been fucking too, and I know what type of dick I want," she said. Once again, Derrick's words had gotten to her. Now she wanted to hurt his little ego.

He shook his head. "That's all you took from what I just said?" he asked. "It's clear you been fucking. Any other time, you don't complain about the dick I'm giving you. If you don't want to be with me, just say that."

Heaven was silent. She couldn't say anything because she didn't really know what she wanted.

"Right!" he said and sat back down on the bed. He picked his phone up and set his alarm. "I'll be up early to drop you off at the airport."

"Derrick," she said, walking into his face. Heaven cradled her arms around Derrick's head and pushed her bare pussy into his face. She knew she was toxic, just like her mother, and she hated it.

"Watch out, Heaven. I don't even want to fuck no more," he said, pushing her back. At this point, his dick was soft, and there was nothing Heaven could say or do to get it back stiff. Derrick loved Heaven, but she was a tough person to be in a relationship with. No matter what he did, whether it was wrong or right, Heaven made him feel like he wasn't doing enough. "Don't do me no favors. I don't want no sympathy pussy." His voice trailed off as he stood up and picked up his towel. He wrapped it back around his waist.

"This ain't no sympathy pussy. This is your pussy, but it's your loss." She walked past him and climbed into bed.

Derrick smirked. "Nah, love. That pussy ain't been mine for a long time… but I'm not trippin'. I won't lose no sleep."

"Derrick, you are so dramatic."

"I'm not, and to show you how much I understand the fact that you're no longer mine, I'ma give you your space and sleep in the guest room. Have a good night."

Heaven rolled her eyes and sucked her teeth. She wasn't about to beg him to stay, and she damn sure was not about to beg him to fuck her. She had bigger things to worry about.

"Okay. Turn the light off on your way out." She threw the covers over her body and made herself comfortable in the middle of the bed, making it clear that she didn't mind sleeping alone.

A couple hours later, as she laid in her bed, tossing and turning, she couldn't believe Derrick had left her the way he did. High and dry, literally. Although she acted as if it didn't bother her, deep down inside it did. Now, she was stuck, woke. For the past few hours, she had been tossing and turning, as if she didn't have to be up in a few hours. Her mind was in overdrive. Every time she was alone, she couldn't help but think. She thought about life so often, and she scolded herself for her mistakes. Her thoughts were what made her want to return to Chicago, Illinois. Tonight, she thought about everything from Derrick and his words about her being toxic and acting just like Anika to how dumb she was for trying to start a relationship with Kash. When it came to her mother, she knew they had similar ways. She didn't need Derrick throwing that fact in her face.

But when it came to Kash, she said, "Maybe he's right. Maybe I am dumb." Yet, Heaven was hardheaded. She had to see for herself.

Sitting up in bed, she looked towards the bedroom door and into the hallway. It was dark as fuck. Scooting over to the nightstand, she saw Derrick's phone laying on top. She figured she'd take it to him, but first her toxic ass decided to look through it. His passcode was simple since they both used the same exact numbers. After the phone was unlocked, Heaven wasted no time. Her fingers moved rapidly as she clicked on app after app, trying to find some type of infidelity so that way she would feel like she wasn't doing anything wrong. Derrick's phone was dry as hell, however. He was too faithful, and Heaven didn't like that. Nothing in his phone was interesting. His text messages were dry, his Facebook messenger was dry, and his call log was even drier. She sucked her teeth.

Removing the covers and standing up, she felt the cold air from the central air hit her body. She still had his phone in her hand and her eyes on the dimly lit screen. She walked towards the bedroom's door. Being sneaky, before exiting the room, she looked both ways down the long hallway, as if she was crossing the street. She walked out and down the hall to the guest room. The door was wide open, as if Derrick was expecting her. The lights were off, and it was silent, but the TV that was on in the bedroom added a brownish hue. She peeped inside and saw his back was facing her.

"Derrick," Heaven said softly as she entered the threshold. He didn't respond. It was clear that he was asleep. "You left your phone in the room." She walked inside and over to the bed. She climbed in behind him and threw the covers over his body. She wrapped her arms around him and kissed his back. "Derrick." He stirred slightly and turned around with his eyes still closed. She wrapped her hand around his dick as she stared into his face. Surprisingly, he was on hard. Afterwards, she kissed his lips. "Derrick." She said his name again.

His eyes slowly fluttered open, and he breathed heavily, panting as Heaven began to work her hand back and forth, massaging his instant stiffness. He put his arm around her and palmed her round ass, kissing her lips back. No apologies were spoken between neither Derrick or Heaven. Her climbing into bed with him was all the necessary sorry he needed.

Heaven was an indecisive person. She didn't know what she wanted in life. Most times, she just went with the flow, and she knew she couldn't leave Atlanta without showing her fiancé some type of love, whether that was a hug or just laying up with him. That was the least she could do. However, here she was, laying on her left side with her right leg now thrown over Derrick's waist as he dug his nails into her thigh, gripping her, making sure she didn't move. He flipped her onto her back and climbed on top. The entire time their lips were still locked.

Now that he knew how she preferred to be fucked, he planned to give her exactly what she wanted. He pulled his lips from hers' and lifted up. He proceeded to lift her legs up, pushing them as far back as they would go. She yelped. He forcefully pushed himself inside her, and she screamed.

"Shut up," he said.

"You shut up," she replied, moaning out in pain.

"Why are you being so rough?"

"You really have to ask why? What did you tell me a few hours ago? Girls your age don't like kissing and shit, right? They like to be banged the fuck out," he stated as he began to work her.

"Derrick," Heaven panted. She fucked up, but she never told him she wanted to lose her walls. Although she didn't want him licking and sucking on her, she didn't want him to fuck her as hard as he was either. He'd never been this rough with her.

"What?" he said aggressively. Already, he was too far gone as he rocked his hips back and forth with just as much aggression.

"Please, slow down," she begged. And although she begged him to slow down, she began to match his strokes, fast and intense. She felt herself going deaf. Digging her long nails into his back, she moaned and shook as she continued to ride the wave of ecstasy.

"Fuck," he grunted, his pace slowing down. He put his lips to her chest and sucked in between her breasts as he came. The room became silent as the headboard stopped knocking, and their sexual sighs ceased. Derrick turned his head to the side and laid in Heaven's chest. He closed his eyes, listening to the sound of her rapid heartbeat.

"That shit was so fucking good." Heaven broke the silence.

"Hell yeah. I ain't never came that fast in my life." He sighed and rolled off of her.

"There's a first time for everyone." She turned on her side to look at him.

"Come here." He pulled her to him and together they fell asleep.

The following morning, Heaven and Derrick were up bright and early. Now that she'd gotten Derrick out the way, it was time to see what was next for her.

FIVE

A thirty-inch, bleach blonde wig, that looked as if it was coming from her scalp, flowed down past her breast and onto her lap as she took her place on the edge of the soft leather seat in first class. Sighing, Heaven fanned her face with her right hand and closed her eyes. She was really about to do this, and she couldn't believe it. After five long years, she was about to step foot in Chicago. She was now finally ready to face her fears. Heaven hadn't even seen her best friend, Esha, in five years because, with everything they had going on with life, neither woman had time to see one another.

Wrapped around her left wrist was an oversized Christian Dior tote, a platinum birthstone bracelet, and a tattoo of her daughter's name. She wore a beige sweatsuit that was at least two size too big for her and a pair of size five glow Yeezy slides on her feet that accentuated her toes and the white polish on her toenails. She scooted back in her seat, and as she looked down to remove her tote bag, she froze in place as her 3.37 carat, excellent cut, round diamond, French cut pavé, diamond engagement ring took over her vision. She flexed her fingers as she chewed on the side of her bottom lip. Heavily, she closed her eyes and let out a deep sigh before removing it and putting it into her pocket. Heaven couldn't believe she agreed to marry one man and was now on her way to chase after another one.

If only things could've been different, she thought as her sweatpants covered thighs and backside slid all the way back into the seat. If only she would've met Derrick first, falling in love with him wouldn't have been an issue.

Oversized blue sunglasses with the name Christian Dior engraved on the sides covered her eyes, and for a second, they became a little misty. Heaven was emotional; however, she wasn't a wreck. She knew she was possibly going on a blank mission, but if things didn't work out between her and Kash, Derrick would still be there to pick up the pieces. Honestly, she didn't like the fact that she had to play with one man's heart to mend her own, but this was currently her life.

Ding! She jumped, and her heart raced as her cellphone dinged, indicating she had a text message. She removed her phone from her tote and smiled, seeing Esha's name. "What does this girl want?" Heaven said to herself, unlocking her phone. Her heart skipped a beat when she clicked on the message icon and saw a picture of Lance and Esha standing next to her baby daddy, Kash.

Well damn! she thought, staring at Kash's sexy ass smirk. He was so damn tall and lean with the same sandy brown hair as Kamelia. His broad chest and shoulders made him look strong. Heaven wanted to climb his tall ass like a tree and wrap her legs around his shoulders. Involuntarily, she licked her lips. Heaven pulled her sunglasses off and placed them inside her tote before placing it underneath the seat in front of her. She knew what Esha was trying to do when she sent that picture. She was trying to scare her ass off the airplane, but she was locked in and ready to live an adventurous life. This was definitely out of the ordinary for her. Plus, the sight of Kash in that moment made her curious. She placed her seatbelt around her waist and sat back comfortably before responding to Esha's text.

Heaven: ??

Esha: Now that I have your attention. LOL

Heaven: LOL. My best friend always has my attention, boo.

Esha: Cut all that best friend shit out, Miss Heaven Wright. It's a damn shame I'm only getting to see you because of this light skinned negro.

Heaven: No, that isn't true, friend. I've invited you to Atlanta on plenty occasions. You know how I felt about Chicago. If I would've ran into that man with another bitch, I would've definitely lost my shit. So, I stayed away.

Esha: You're making excuses.

Heaven: I'm not!

Esha: What if you see him with a bitch when you get here? All the ladies love Kash.

Heaven: Idk. I haven't thought about that.

Esha: Well, friend, are you ready?

Heaven: Yes, love. I'm on the plane now, nervous as fuck.

Esha: Suck it up, buttercup. I can't wait to see you. It's been too fucking long.

Heaven: I knoooow, but I just couldn't stomach the thought of seeing Kashmir. A bitch is grown as hell now, and he's either gonna be my man or I'ma kill him. LOL

Esha: Girl. LOL.

Heaven: So, all his little hoes need to move around, shawty. Big Heaven is on her way to stake her claim.

Esha: Period, friend.

She let Esha have the last word before getting trapped in her own thoughts. For the next fifteen minutes, Heaven couldn't contain her feelings. Her moods were apparent. Everything she felt showed on her face, from how excited she was to her fears.

She couldn't wait to see Esha and the new apartment in downtown Chicago her father had gotten for her. Any other time, Heaven would've just stayed at Reign's childhood home in Park Ridge, a suburb northwest of Chicago, but she knew she would need her own space, just in case her and Kash decided to rekindle their unspoken feelings from the past.

The safety check announcement came alive on the overhead speaker, and Heaven took a deep breath.

"Lord, I pray I'm doing the right thing. Not only for me but for Kamelia too," she said silently. "Shoot, just get me to Chicago and back home safely, and that will be enough confirmation for me." She looked down into her phone once again and sent her father, Derrick, Reign, and Anika a quick group message, letting them know her flight was now leaving.

Heaven: Okay, y'all. I'm getting ready to take off. Send a quick prayer up for me.

Afterwards, she put her phone on airplane mode. Placing her AirPods inside her ears to drown out the noises surrounding her with a movie she'd found on Tubi, she laid back and tried her best to focus on the urban film. Not really wanting to hear anything the captain had to say, because that announcement would only make things official, she turned the volume all the way up.

The lights dimmed, and the plane began to shake just as badly as her shivering, nervous body. "Oh my God!" She bit down on her bottom lip. "I'm really about to do this." She couldn't contain herself. Sitting up slightly to look around, she smiled. She was alone. For the first time ever in life, she was traveling miles and miles away from home by herself. No Mommy, no Daddy, no Kamelia, no Derrick, no Delilah, no Reign, no KeKe, no King, nobody, just herself and a bunch of passengers she didn't know. Everyone aboard looked relaxed and content, even the beautiful young lady, who looked about her age, sitting to the left of her with a newborn baby latched on to her breast. Her face was beat past the Gods, and Heaven wondered how she was able to look so pretty with a baby hanging on to her left nipple. Heaven figured she had to be on her way to claim what was hers as well.

Welcome aboard Delta flight DL 1374. This is a nonstop flight from Atlanta to Chicago… She heard the announcement loud and clear as she removed one earbud from her ear. She was on her way, and there was no turning back. This shit better be worth her while because she would hate herself so much if she came back home empty handed. Although Kamelia had never asked about her father, she felt that was the least she could do, initiate a relationship between Kash and Kamelia.

The plane began to move slowly, and seconds later, it picked up speed. It soared down the runway as ecstatic butterflies danced around her stomach. Soon enough, the plane was lifting from the ground and hovering over homes and establishments. She watched in amazement as she always did whenever she took flight. Soon enough, her eyes were fixated on the passing clouds as she thought about Derrick and how she would tell him she'd found someone else. She knew he would be hurt, but she had to do what was best for her.

SIX

Asia lay with her head resting up against Kash's chest, and her eyes were closed tightly, reflecting on her past. She grew up in a loving home with both parents and two older brothers, but you would never guess that from the type of woman she turned out to be. She knew how her adulthood would turn out. She didn't have a go getter's mentality like the rest of her family, so she had done the bare minimum in both elementary and high school. She had done just enough to graduate. Knowing that her education wasn't going to get her anywhere far at an early age, she knew how she would maintain the lifestyle her parents provided. She was unlike her family. She was the black sheep and the rebellious one out of her siblings.

"Count your fucking days in my house, Asia." She remembered her mother saying to her after a heated argument. It was her senior year in high school, and she was failing terribly. "You know, it is truly a shame that you don't care about your education. Your brothers are almost out of college, doing very well, but you… No! You want to be a dumb ass. You will be eighteen soon, and I want you gone. You don't want shit out of life, and I don't need the ignorance around me. I hate to say or see it, but you're gonna struggle. I just hope you don't bring any kids into this world."

She rolled her eyes at the memory and sucked her teeth. She had to be honest with herself. Her mother was right. Without a man, life for Asia would definitely be a struggle.

Asia was a miserable woman but very strategic. Every man she ever wanted, she got them through manipulation or, as she called it, being in the right place at the right time. Still, every man she ever tried to settle down with used her for sex, and in return, she used them for their money. She reasoned that even exchange wasn't robbery.

Three beautiful kids came from these short-lived relationships, but she felt as if she received the short end of the stick. She birthed the kids and lost the man.

At the age of twenty-five with three kids, you would think she would have her shit together, but that was not the case. Asia had nothing but a three-bedroom low income townhome and a 2018 Subaru Impreza her second baby daddy helped her lease with a high ass APR in which Kash now footed the note. Three good for nothing baby daddies and a simple ass mind.

Her two oldest children's fathers were big time drug dealers; however, they contributed absolutely nothing towards Malaysia and India's life. And this fact was all Asia's fault. Being the bum bitch she was, after they found out she had nothing to offer but pussy and a smart mouth, they quickly realized she wasn't worth the headache, and neither was the baby they created together. But her son's father did what he could, which wasn't much. It was by chance she stumbled upon Kash. They had followed one another for years on social media, yet they never really interacted. Asia was on the prowl, trying to bait her a money-making nigga. She posted a thirst trap picture on her page and in her story. After Kash slid in her DMs, the rest was history.

Asia was a very beautiful girl. She just lacked ambition. She had no real goals or aspirations. Asia just lived life in the moment. Although she chose men who didn't work an honest job, they were men who had enough money to allow her to live comfortably. Their ambitions were beyond working for the white man. They were simply forced and focused on making sure their family and the people around them ate. Asia was something like a trophy to these types of men. She possessed body and beauty, but she was a birdbrain. She for sure wasn't offering anything long term because she didn't have anything to offer to anyone, not even her three kids.

Her oldest child, Malaysia, was only six years old

but was something like a surrogate mother to her four-year-old sister, India, and one-year-old brother, Taiwan. Unlike Asia, her children weren't privy to a caring mother nor were they privy to seeing their mother in a stable relationship. Asia bounced from man to man. Kash had been the longest relationship she'd had in a while, with her relationship with Taiwan's father coming in second place. So, her kids were well aware of the revolving door her home possessed.

"Kashmir," she whispered, feeling behind herself, above her head, and placing her hand to Kash's face.

He sucked his teeth, stirring slightly. "Come on, G." He moved his face back.

"What?" she asked, offended.

"You know I don't like mufuckas touching my face." Kash was definitely on his light skinned shit. Getting back to his slumber, he closed his eyes, and almost instantly, he was snoring and slobbering.

Asia sighed. With the sun beginning to peep through the curtains, she had to make sure he was still there. She turned to look at him. Muffing him softly in his head, she knew he was pretending to be sleep.

"You ain't give me no dick last night, but you wanna be up in here telling me I can't touch you," she said. It was almost as if she was talking to herself because Kash still had his eyes closed. He spoke no words. He just snored loudly. He was balled up in a fetal position with his hands clasped and his fingers intertwined together in between his knees. "Kashmir, you hear me talking to you. You must be fucking someone else." She sucked her teeth. "There's no way you should've been denying this pussy after not seeing me in two weeks."

"Huh, Asia, believe what you want to believe, just shut the fuck up. I'm tryna get some sleep. I gotta get up in a few." He grabbed her around her waist and pulled her to him, thinking this gesture would definitely quiet her, and he could get a couple more hours of sleep. "Cool out, man. I'ma fuck you later, shorty. After my basketball game… Oh shit, and after I check on this lil' situation for Dre. I got you."

"Okay," Asia smiled at him, allowing him to pull her body closer. She was satisfied with his statement. Asia was happy Kash recognized why she was upset and was willing to make it right.

Almost instantly, his eyes were closed, his mind drifted off into lala land, and his mouth was wide open, so she kissed him.

"Dry ass lips."

Kash was knocked out sleep again. And as he fell into an even deeper sleep, she reached for her phone. Knowing he would be out for at least another hour, she decided to take a few snapshots. Holding him around his neck and cradling his head, she put her face on top of his and put her lips to his ear as she took multiple pictures.

"To love or be loved! Mr. Kashmir Harris, who are you dreaming about?" Asia whispered as she typed a question mark at the end of a status, along with one of the pictures she'd just taken of herself and a sleeping Kashmir, posting on Instagram. From everything that happened the day before with his cousin, Nadia, Asia quickly came to the conclusion that Kash had a bunch of hoes, especially after Nadia let the words venomously slip from her mouth. It wasn't connecting with Asia that Nadia had said it just to piss her off, so she needed to make sure every bitch in Chicago, hell the entire world, knew who the fuck she was. She was his woman, the chick he spent his time with whenever it was convenient for him.

In her heart, she knew another bitch had his attention after he'd gone missing for two weeks, so after posting their picture, she spent $60 of Kash's money to boost her post, making sure it circulated social media rapidly. Turning her back to him and pushing her ass up against him, she laid in his arms. This was the best feeling in the world, and she wished they could lay like this forever. She knew Kash didn't love her. Hell, she didn't love him either. Their relationship was still brand new, still she loved everything Kashmir did for her. Life wouldn't be possible right now if it wasn't for him.

She exhaled and sent a text to her oldest daughter, telling her to get her siblings and bring them into her bedroom. Minutes later, when the kids finally opened the door and walked inside, Asia told them all to get into the bed. She had some trickery up her sleeve.

"Lay behind your step daddy, Malaysia and India," she said in a whisper. "Hurry up… Taiwan, come lay right here in front of Mommy." Her tone was still low.

With her one-year-old laying in front of her and the other two laying behind Kash, they looked like the perfect family. Now, they were all in position. "One, two, three, say cheeeeessse!" She snapped the picture. This one wasn't going to hit social media just yet. Instead, she planned to keep it in her back pocket, knowing one day soon she would have to use it.

Kash didn't have a Facebook or Instagram anymore, so she didn't worry about him seeing the sneaky shit she was up to. Even if he did find out, he was her man, and she shouldn't be a secret. He was a man hard to get next to, so why not show the world whose bed he slept in most nights?

"Alright, y'all can get the fuck out now," she said as she sat up and put her baby boy, little Taiwan, on the floor. Asia was so bitter. She didn't care how she talked to her children or how she made them feel. Scrunching up her nose and frowning after getting a whiff of Taiwan's nasty diaper, she turned on her back and propped herself up on her pillow, so she could get a clear view of her daughters. "Look at his damn pamper," she yelled as Malaysia and India walked to the foot of the bed. "What the hell did I tell y'all about letting your little brother walk around here pissy and shitty? You two are so fucking nasty. Especially you Malaysia. You know better. You're the oldest. You're supposed to look out for your brother and sister."

"I was about to change him, but you texted me," she said in a timid voice.

"I don't give a fuck who texted you, whether it was me on Jesus Christ himself. Let me catch Taiwan like this again, and I'ma fuck you up."

Tears began to well up in Malaysia's eyes. This type of treatment was normal for her. Asia acted as if these kids were her responsibility.

"Wipe your damn eyes, Malaysia. I got my man over here, and you let your little brother come in here like this. Now my room smells like a skunk," Asia said, going on a rant. Until she was suddenly silenced.

"Man, what the fuck you screaming at these kids about early in the morning?"

"Nothing. Y'all get the fuck outta my room, and Malaysia, change your brother's pamper." As the kids left the room, she looked at the time on her phone. It was a little after 8:30 in the morning, too early to be having this conversation with Malaysia.

"You need to stop talking to them like that, G. I try not to get in your business as a mother, so don't do that shit around me."

"Kash," she said. Turning, she put her hand to his chest and looked him in his eyes. Her eyes were pleading. She didn't want to hear anything he had to say about the way she treated her kids, especially Malaysia because her father was who did Asia the dirtiest.

"Nah, man. What type of mother are you?" he asked as he prayed Heaven was nothing like Asia.

Asia sucked her teeth. "I'm still learning, Kash. My mother didn't really show me how to be a woman or mother."

"I have a daughter…" he announced but was cut off by Asia's loud, obnoxious voice.

"You have a daughter?" she asked. "Why is this the first time I'm hearing about your daughter, Kash? Why haven't you brought her around? Am I not good enough to meet your precious baby? Who the fuck is your baby mama? It's probably that bogus, inflatable bitch, Nadia. I knew she wasn't your cousin, Kashmir." Question after question shot from her mouth. Her eyes turned red as tears attempted to fill her brims. Kash shook his head.

"Man, you worried about the wrong shit. Stay focused on what I'm saying to you. I have a daughter, and the way I see you treating Malaysia makes me wonder if my baby mama doing the same shit. But I pray she know better than to test me like that. Malaysia is only six, and my daughter is five."

"Kash, you have a five-year-old daughter? When were you going to tell me? After we were married and had kids of our own?"

"Married? Kids of our own? You going too far. Listen, lil lady, your daughter shouldn't be mothering her siblings. That's your job. We could never have a shorty together. That's why I make sure I strap up every time I fuck you. You let these niggas knock you up and dip. Now you taking the shit out on your kids. They didn't do it. You chose these fucked up individuals to have kids with." He moved her hand from his chest and swung the covers from his body before standing up. He reached down to the floor and picked up his clothes from the night before and quickly began to get dressed as Asia sat there, looking stupid.

"I don't take anything out on them," she lied. In all honesty, after she lost the man, she was no longer interested in being a mother to the kid. They were only a reminder of what should've been. Now, Kash, on the other hand, he was great with her kids. The perfect father. She wanted to trap him so bad. She wanted to have a whole football team by him. Asia knew Kash would never turn his back on his own kids considering how passionately he spoke about her own relationship with her kids. "You don't want any kids with me,

Kash?"

"Hell naw. Why would I? I will kill you over mine. Shit, you make me wanna call DCFS on your ass at times." Asia's mothering skills disgusted Kash.

"So, that's why you pretended to be so drunk last night? You didn't have any condoms."

"I wasn't pretending shit. I was really fucked up, but no, I didn't have any condoms either. I don't need pussy that bad."

"I'm working on it, Kash… I'm working on myself as a person and mother," she said as she got on her hands and knees in bed and crawled to the foot.

"You don't have to explain nothing to me. Go explain that to the three kids that is sitting in the living room waiting on a home cooked meal. Your kids need your attention and explanation more than I do." He began walking to the bedroom's door. "You seem to love me more than you love them, and I don't agree with that shit." He walked out the room.

Asia huffed as the bedroom door shut. She fell out on her back in the middle of her bed and sulked. This nigga had a child. A five-year-old daughter whom he clearly didn't know anything about, but he could sit and tell her he didn't want any kids by her. The entire time, Asia thought he didn't want to bring any kids into the world because of his lifestyle. She never made a big deal about him not wanting to be with her intimately without a condom. But to know he had a child, a fucking five-year-old daughter, told a story of its own.

Tears clouded her vision and ran from the corners of her eyes, onto the sides of her face, and down onto the silver silk sheets on her bed. She needed some questions answered. Now, she was past confused. She wondered if he was somewhere being a family man with his child, his five-year-old daughter, and his daughter's mother when he was gone for weeks. She wondered if he was still fucking her raw and how often. Finding out about his child, his damn five-year-old daughter, right now just did something to her. She wanted to kill Kash's baby mama and his child.

Ten minutes had passed, and Asia still lay in the same exact spot Kash had left her in, still in tears and in her own head about where her and Kashmir's relationship stood. Nothing about the way she acted towards her kids bothered her. It was normal for her to treat them that way. But Kash, that was a whole other story.

The doorknob twisted, and Kash walked inside to retrieve his shoes. "Aye, drop me off at my car," he said as he put one size thirteen foot into a pair of all white Air Force Ones.

"No." She sat up, folded her arms across her chest, and looked at Kash with her bottom lip poked out.

"What you mean no?" Kash walked over to her. Reaching out to her, he grabbed her elbow and pulled her to him. "What's wrong?" Wrapping his arms around her, Kash put his face into Asia's neck, kissing her softly.

"Kash," she whined.

"Yes," he said with his lips still up against her neck.

Kash's warm breath up against Asia's flesh made her tremble slightly. Her eyes closed, and her breathing became labored. It was weird how he just went from telling her she could never be anything more than just a fuck buddy or a little girlfriend, and now, here he was, trying to cater to her feelings.

Kash forced his weight down on Asia, forcing her to lay down on the bed as he climbed on top of her with his lips still against her neck.

"Instead of me dropping you off at your car, I can just go to your game with you," she said, but he didn't respond. "I can be your little cheerleader… Go, Kash, go." She giggled as he chuckled.

"I'm supposed to meet up with Lance in an hour so we can ride to the game together. I got something to do after my game too."

"Okay, that's fine. We can meet up with Lance and then I can take you to your car afterwards. We never do anything in public together. I feel like I'm your secret."

"You're not my secret, Asia. I fucks with you the long way."

"Prove it." If she couldn't have his baby, he had to prove that they were locked in for the long haul. She was tired of people not knowing who he belonged to.

"Get dressed. Get the kids dressed too."

"The kids can stay home. I'll pay for a babysitter to come over," Asia said, just in case she had to act an ass at the basketball court.

"Okay." He walked over to her dresser drawers and located a pair of basketball shorts, T-shirt, and boxers. Taking his shoes back off, Kash went to the bathroom to get dressed.

S E V E N

"Best friend!" Heaven yelled into the phone as soon as Esha said hello. She'd just landed in Chicago not even five minutes ago, and she was excited. Before the wheels could even touch the ground, Heaven was powering her phone back on. She was uncontainable. The rush of seeing the outside of O'Hare International Airport as they rolled past the other aircrafts let her know that shit was about to get real. She'd never been one to chase after a man, but hey, you only lived once.

"Heaven!" Esha yelled excitedly. "Are you here? In Chicago?"

"Yes, bish!" Heaven laughed. Esha screamed into the receiver and so did Heaven. Their voices boomed, disturbing the peace and serenity of first class.

"Mmm mmm!" A passenger cleared her throat aloud, and Heaven turned to see who the attention seeking bitch was.

"Girrrrl!" she yelled, eyebrows meeting in the

center of her forehead in a ugly frown. Clearly something in first class smelled foul because Heaven's scowl told it all. "This bitch might wanna swallow that nut she just coughed up."

"Who?"

"Some lady on this plane. In here clearing her throat like that's gonna shut me the fuck up." Heaven was so loud that the passengers around her stared, but she could care less.

"Stop, friend," Esha said, laughing. "They're gonna ban your ass from the airport."

"My daddy will buy this airplane and airport. The hell," Heaven said while looking in the lady's direction.

A stewardess came over and asked Heaven to keep her voice down as the captain was giving instructions for exiting the plane.

"Girl, let me hurry up and get off this plane before I be in jail," she laughed. "What you doing? You better either be here or on your way because I'm ready to get out in these streets," Heaven said.

"Girl, who said I was coming to pick you up?"

"Esha, stop playing with me."

"You better go get your spoiled ass on the Blueline or in a Lyft," Esha said in a serious tone. "I don't do the airport."

"Blueline? A Lyft?" Heaven's nose was turned up.

"Esha, stop playing with me." She ran her fingers through her wig.

"Naw, let me stop playing with my friend. Bitch, you already know I'm outside waiting on you." Esha laughed, and Heaven squealed, screaming excitedly.

The lady that held a newborn baby, that sat across from Heaven, looked at her curiously, as if to tell her to shut the fuck up. Heaven saw the expression on her face but didn't say anything. She just pursed her lips together and continued her conversation.

"Anyways, let me get off this phone."

"Why, what happened?"

"This bitch looking at me all crazy and shit. And now her little bald headed ass baby is crying," Heaven whispered, scowling in the lady's direction.

"Okay, boo," she laughed. "Just hurry up. Love ya!"

"Love you too."

Fifteen minutes later, Heaven was walking outside with a cart attendant hot on her trail as he pulled her suitcases outside. Pulling her sunglasses up slightly, with her head on a swivel, she looked for Esha's car.

Heaven pulled her phone from her bag.

"Where is this girl?" she said as she called Esha's phone. It went straight to voicemail, and Heaven sighed. She smacked her lips and turned her head to look at the cart attendant. "I'm sorry. My ride was supposed to been out here."

"It's cool," the young man said, licking his lips as he stared at Heaven's ass. "Aye, you got a decent ass accent. Where you from?"

"A decent accent?" Heaven frowned.

"Yeah." He bit down on his bottom lip flirtatiously. "You got a decent body too."

"Thank you. I think." Quickly, Heaven turned her head back around, focusing on the passing and parked cars.

"Damn, lil mama," the cart attendant said under his breath, but Heaven heard him. She smirked and shook her head. He was a cutie, but she was raised to go for men who could match or go over and beyond her means. A man who could give her the world and then some.

Beep! Beep! The horn blared as a Lexus RX 450 hybrid pulled up and parked directly in front of Heaven. Slow R&B music boomed obnoxiously as a soft, beautiful voice crooned over the bass, making the doors shake. The windows were tinted, so she couldn't see inside. But when the windows came down, Heaven's mouth opened widely, excited to see a familiar face.

"Miss Heaven Wright!" Turning her blinkers on, Esha hurriedly opened the driver's door, stepped out, and ran around the SUV to get to Heaven.

"Oh my God!" Heaven screamed as her and Esha embraced, hugging each other tightly. Tears graced both of their faces rapidly and abundantly while they rocked from side to side.

"Damn, both of y'all decent as hell." He licked his lips.

"Decent? Why do you keep saying that?" Heaven asked. "Is that like a compliment or something?" Her southern twang was so cute as she laughed.

"Hell yeah that's a compliment, shorty," he said, causing Esha to frown, She wasn't impressed at all while Heaven laughed, amused by the guy's attempt at being charming.

"Girl, you know how these niggas are nowadays. They don't know how to use complimentary words like beautiful or pretty. Instead, they say dumb shit like decent." She rolled her eyes.

"I love that attitude shit, lil' lady."

"Do I look like a little lady to you?" Esha asked.
"Nigga, you at work. Pretend like you know how to beprofessional."

"Esha!" Heaven laughed. "Okay, you're upsetting my best friend. Just grab my bags and put them in the trunk. I have a decent tip for you," Heaven said, laughing.

"My bad, love." He offered an apology to Esha.

"Boy! Just put her bags in the trunk." Esha scowled as she and Heaven began walking towards the truck. Esha tapped a button on her car key that made the trunk door open.

"So, y'all best friends? You got an attitude and shit, but I like that. Both of y'all need to take my number down. Shit, we can all be friends, you feel me? Both of y'all slug bug around this bitch. Bootylicious like a mufucka." He began lifting her bags into the trunk as they stood there watching him. Heaven and Esha laughed at his comment.

"You are so funny, but I'm taken, and so is she. So, your phone number ain't going no where near my damn phone," Esha said and walked off to the driver's door.

"You are hilarious," Heaven smiled, going into her bag and pulling out her wallet. "Thank you, sir." She handed him two fifty-dollar bills.

"Thanks, lil baby. Can I get your phone number too?"

"Nah, I can't give you my phone number." She

smiled, raising her left hand to show her engagement ring, forgetting that she had removed it while she was on the plane.

"What does that mean?" he asked.

"Oh shit." She felt inside her pocket and put her ring back on. "I'm engaged. I can't have men calling my phone," she said, smiling. This guy didn't realize he didn't stand a chance with Heaven. Or maybe he did but wasn't going away that easy.

"Tell that nigga I'm yo' lil cousin."

"He knows my entire family." Her left eyebrow rose.

"Yo' big forehead ass making a lot of excuses."

Heaven put her hand to her head and scoffed. She was fake offended. "My forehead is not big, but I'm not making excuses. I am engaged, and my fiancé will have a fit."

"Your fiancé is back in Atlanta, right? Come hang out with the kid. I can just show you around Chicago this weekend."

"No, thanks, but I appreciate the offer. Enjoy your day, sir." Heaven walked off as the trunk began to close.

"Man, that fake ass ring, shorty!" he yelled. Heaven laughed as she continued to walk to the front passenger's side.

As soon as she climbed inside the truck, she blew out a breath. Heaven and Esha looked at one another and burst out laughing. Esha was the asshole of the two while Heaven had so much southern hospitality. She was so sweet and polite. She would've felt bad talking crazy to the guy the way Esha did.

"You really stood there and talked to his dusty ass? You better not had gave him your number."

"I didn't. But I didn't want to be mean. He was decent," Heaven said, and they both laughed.

"Come here, boo. Give me a hug," Esha said, reaching her arms out to Heaven. They embraced, and suddenly the two women were full of tears "I missed you so much, friend."

"I missed you too. You're my big sister."

"We let five years pass us by like that. Don't ever let you not wanting to be around a nigga keep us apart again. And I promise I will come to Atlanta and visit you."

"I won't. I missed your baby shower, not wanting to run into Kash," Heaven said as Esha pulled back slightly and used her thumbs to wipe Heaven's tears.

"We've both missed a lot." Esha wiped her own tears. The sounds of whining caused both ladies to turn their heads to the backseat.

"Esha, you didn't tell me you had my nephew with you," she smiled. She got on her knees in her seat and reached behind her. Esha's four-month-old baby, Lance Jr., was so fat and juicy. He was so cute with his baby afro and chubby cheeks. As he began to stir from his sleep, he threw punches and kicked his little feet. "He is so cute. Hey, my little phew phew." Heaven touched his toes. Instantly, little Lance opened his eyes and looked at Heaven curiously. His bottom lip poked out before a handsome smile took over his face.

"Oh my God, Esha. He has a dimple like me. Him is so sexy," Heaven said in a baby voice. Picking up his pacifier from his lap, she put it into his mouth before turning around in her seat and putting her seatbelt on.

EIGHT

Asia walked through the crowd of people in the outdoor basketball court to the top of the bleachers. Standing there with dark sunglasses pulled over her eyes, she peeped her surroundings. On the right side of her sat two beautiful women who were clearly there looking for a man. The way they were dressed was quite provocative. It was the same way Asia dressed when she was looking for attention. With a pink fitted romper on that showed both her pussy print and her round, voluptuous ass, the woman who sat next to Asia tried to stand out from the rest. Asia scowled because the women made her stomach churn. She appeared to be in her early twenties with beautiful, chocolate cocoa brown skin, and her friend looked just as beautiful. Asia could see Kash going for women like them, and it was obvious the thirst was very fucking real. Surely they came to these games to get chosen.

"Hey, girl. Ooouuu, you are too cute," the girl that sat the closest to her said. "I ain't never seen you out here before. Who you here with?"

"Mmm, thanks. I'm here with my man." With a stank look on her face, Asia looked at the two women as if they were beneath her. It was true. She didn't fuck with females at all because she knew they all wanted her nigga. She even cut her best friend off as soon as her and Kash began talking. She saw her as competition, and she couldn't have her around him.

Friendly ass bitch. Her pussy probably just as friendly. Nuh uhn, Asia, you gotta keep your eyes on this bitch, she thought.

"I love pretty bitches. Ou, look at your hair. It's so long and shiny." Asia could barely take a seat before this girl was all in her face. She grimaced. She was so far up Asia's ass that she considered finding another seat. "Where do you get your bundles from?" The girl touched Asia's hair, and Asia moved her head as her long tresses fell from the girl's hand.

"Wait a minute. I'm not with that gay shit," Asia announced, still mugged up. "These ain't no damn bundles. This is all me. But again, thank you." A half smirk was on her face.

"I'm not gay either, bitch. A beautiful woman can't compliment another woman? I'm just tryna give you your props. Calm yo' ass down."

"I said thank you the first time. You're acting like you wanna eat my ass." Asia had a smart-ass mouth.

"Girl!" The girl rolled her eyes and looked in the

opposite direction at her friend. "Anyways."

"I can't stand a stuck-up ass hoe," the other girl whispered while frowning. She made sure not to say it out loud. Asia looked like she was ready to fight, and with a mouth like hers, she could probably get down with the best of them. "That's why I don't be complimenting bitches."

"Tell me about it." She shook her head and quietly looked ahead at the men on the court. It was weird to her how women took compliments from other women with an attitude. She had nothing left to say to Asia.

Asia made herself comfortable on the wooden seats next to the friendly bitch and watched her man run up and down the outdoor court as he and Lance warmed up. He looked so sexy from the way he dribbled the basketball to the way he ran to the free throw line. Kash was more than a few inches taller than Lance and the other two men they were playing against, and it made this game almost impossible for them to lose. Asia was hoping to be Kash's good luck charm, seeing as though he and Lance were playing for 20,000 dollars. He had never been selfish with his money, so if he won, she knew he would share at least a thousand dollars with her.

"That's one fine ass nigga there," she said in a low tone. She was trapped in her own head, blocking the whole world out. Her vision was tunneled as she speculated and watched Kash intently.

"Bianca, girl, look at that tall ass nigga right there," Asia distinctly heard the girl who she exchanged words with say, but she seemed in the distance. "This bitch asking me am I gay when I come to these games every mufuckin' Saturday just to see him. He is just too fine for words," she said, giving her friend a high five.

After coming to a game two months ago with her cousin and seeing the handsome Kashmir, who appeared to be single because he never brought a woman here with him, she'd come back every single week to watch Kash and Lance's games, praying that one day soon he would say something to her.

"Yes, friend. I wonder if he has a girl. What is his real name? I'm about to search for him on Facebook. A nigga's social media page will tell you everything you need to know about him." Bianca pulled her phone out and went to her Facebook app, awaiting her friend's response.

"I don't know his real name, but everybody out here calls him Killa K. Girl, we ain't gon' find shit on social media typing in the name Killa K. You know they make you put your real name on there now."

Asia turned her head to look at them. She cocked her head, wondering if they were talking about her Killa K. Now she was out of her head and all ears.

"I've never seen him with anyone. But I know a man that delicious looking can't be single."

"Why not? Even if he isn't single, you acting like you ain't never fucked with another bitch's nigga. Shit, if you're scared to talk to him, I will."

"Now you know damn well I'm not scared."

"You sure?"

"Positive. I'ma give him some congratulations pussy after this game," Jessica laughed.

"That's my bitch!" Bianca laughed as well.

Asia knew it was a reason she didn't like the bitches; nevertheless, she was happy that she had sat here. As she listened to the two women adoring her man, she wondered how many other women were there to ogle lustfully at Kash. Silently, she smiled, trying her best to stay composed. She didn't want to embarrass Kash in public. He made his feeling clear yesterday. He didn't like her acting out in public. Her starting a ruckus in this type of setting just wouldn't be right. But the two women sitting next to her better watch their words. Earlier she boosted a post of her and Kash that she was sure was making its rounds around social media. So, the suspense of who he was fucking with wouldn't be a mystery for too long.

The game was set for four quarters, each timed at ten-minutes, and Asia was prepared to be Kash and Lance's personal cheerleader. The game began, and Asia was locked in. She was that supportive girlfriend, making sure the peanut gallery knew whose team she was rooting for. Every time Kash or Lance got their hands on the basketball, she would jump up and clap her hands, even if they were only touching the ball to pass it to the other team.

Asia was so embarrassing, screaming out, "Let's go! Laces down, hike! Y'all can do it!" every now and then.

"I wish this bitch would shut the fuck up," the two girls who sat on the side of her would whisper.

It was six seconds left on the clock at the end of the fourth quarter, and both teams were tied. On pins and needles, everyone watched as Lance threw the basketball to Kash, and he took a three-point shot. When the ball hit the inside of the rim and danced around the net, the crowd jumped up excitedly as Kash ran backward with his arm raised and wrist bent, still in formation. The ball fell through, giving Team Kash and Lance the winning points. Kash looked up into the audience, making eye contact with Asia, he winked at her. She smiled bashfully and gathered her things. She put her sunglasses on as she heard the two Kash admirers talking.

"Oh my God, Jessica, did you see him winking at you?"

"Yes, bitch." They both began to gather their things as well.

Asia took her time, allowing the two women to

walk out before her, just so she could make them both look stupid. When they began to descend the stairs, Asia was right behind them. The two women walked over to Kash and Lance, congratulating them and of course flirting.

"Congratulations, baby." Asia walked up, pushing Jessica out the way. She wrapped her arms around his waist as he wrapped his arms around her body. Because she was wrapped up in Kash's arms, she couldn't see Jessica or Bianca's faces, but she was sure they were both looking ugly as fuck. The nerve of this bitch, thinking she was about to give Kash anything. What Asia really wanted to do was act a fool, but she didn't want to give Kash an excuse to do him.

NINE

The west side of Chicago was lit as Esha took Heaven down the blocks of her old neighborhood where Lance's mother still lived, allowing her to see how impoverished Black Chicagoans lived. Of course Heaven knew nothing about that way of life, and it saddened her to see the run down neighborhood.

Being sensitive yet curious, Heaven kept her eyes on the people standing outside. The drug addicts were having nasally conversations while they leaned and swayed back and forth, seemingly not able to control their movements. It was obvious they were high as fuck. Heaven knew Sno wouldn't approve of her being in this part of town, but this was where Esha once lived, and she wanted to see. To experience a day in the life of her best friend. Plus, she didn't want to insult Esha or make her feel bad about where she came from.

Although the neighborhood looked like shit, aside from the drug fiends, the people who hung on the corners and near the liquor stores were dressed in the finest labels - Fendi, Gucci, Prada, Burberry, Hermès, and Chanel, all of which looked counterfeit to Heaven, but who was she to judge? She just rode in silence as Esha pointed out specific things, and Lance Jr. cooed in the backseat. She made a mental note to call her father and mother later. She needed them to know how much she appreciated them. In every state, there was a hood, and Heaven knew this for a fact. Although Anika was a toxic, crazy bitch, she made sure Heaven never had to witness life in anything less than beautiful homes with manicured lawns.

"It has to be fun living in the hood," Heaven said as she looked out the passenger's window.

"I've lived in the hood most of my life and let me be the first to tell you it ain't nothing fun about hearing gunshots almost every night. But if you want, I can ask Lance mama to let you stay the night in his sister's old bedroom," Esha laughed.

"Okay, friend. Ask her." Heaven looked over at Esha and raised one eyebrow. "Let me experience the real Chi-town."

"Your daddy got you living downtown. In the heart of the city. That is where you belong. You have too much money to be tryna lay your head in the slums. I won't even lay my head over here. Moving to the suburbs has spoiled the hell out of me. So, Heaven, I know your prissy self wouldn't last one night in this neighborhood. And because you're like my little sister, I would not set you up for failure."

"You have no idea how much of a G I really am. I came from a bloodline of gangstas from both my mother and father's side. You better know when I'm home in Atlanta, I keep a strap on me and a few goons by my side."

"You should've brought that damn strap to Chicago then. And until you decide to link with Kashmir, you ain't got no goons by your side. Not to get it twisted, I'm a real nigga, but I don't fuck with guns," Esha said, laughing as she pulled up in front of a small, brown, bricked home. The porch set high with what seemed like a thousand flowerpots full of green, leafy plants sitting on top of the brick banister.

"Whose house is this?"

"Lance mama, Miss Anita." Esha put her truck in park. "Do you want to meet her? Or are you staying out here?"

"Depends on how long you're gonna be."

"Not long. I just need to pick something up and take baby Lance inside to see his granny." Esha smiled as she turned to look at her baby.

"Maybe you can introduce me another time. I'm not presentable right now," Heaven said, running her fingers through her hair.

"Okay, I'll leave the truck running then. Lance should be pulling up soon." Esha stepped from the car, walked around to the back door, and opened it. She pulled her baby from inside and placed him on her hip. Heaven watched the two as Esha sauntered up the walkway and then the stairs before she pulled her phone out and called Sno.

The phone rang a couple times before she heard Kamelia's excited voice.

"Hey, my love." Heaven smiled. She was equally excited to hear her baby's voice. This was the first time ever she'd had so much distance between herself and Kamelia.

"Hey, Mama. Are you back home yet? I'm almost ready to come home."

Heaven laughed. "No, baby girl. I just made it to Chicago. I won't be back home for a while."

"Awww, man," she sulked.

"Aren't you having fun with DJ and Regan?"

"Yeah, but I miss you."

"Awwww, Kamelia. I miss you too, but Reign and Papa will call me whenever you want to talk to me. Okay?"

"Okay."

The phone went silent as Kamelia's words made Heaven's heart cry, and tears dropped from her eyes. She sniffled.

"Mommy, are you okay?" Kamelia asked.

"Yes, I'm okay." Heaven wiped her eyes.

"Uhm, Mommy… Delilah told me you were leaving me to find my new daddy. She said Grandma Anika told her that," she said, and Heaven shook her head. She could only imagine the way Delilah delivered that news to Kamelia. It was crazy how Anika's messiness rubbed off on her nine-year-old sister. Heaven wasn't going to lie to Kamelia, but at the same time, she wasn't ready for her to know about Kash.

Heaven sighed. "I am in Chicago to talk to your father. I want you guys to have a relationship. He's no one new though."

"I have a father already, Ma."

"I know, babes. But we will talk about everything as soon as I get back home," she said, finding it very hard to have this conversation with Kamelia over the phone. She didn't want to confuse her. Anika's name always seemed to be in the middle of mess. She was one messy bitch. How dare she speak her business to Delilah? What gave her that right? Heaven was pissed. No one knew about the purpose of this trip but Sno, Reign, and somehow Derrick stumbled upon this information.

"Okay."

"I love you, babes."

"I love you too, Mama," Kamelia said.

With the phone still to her ear, she faintly heard Kamelia's voice as she ran away from the phone in search of Sno. "Papa, Papa."

Heaven hung her head, not really sure of how to feel. On one hand, she was able to breathe more because this entire Chicago trip was no longer a secret, still she should've been the one to tell Kamelia. What if she took it upon herself and told her father that Anika was keeping Delilah's paternity a secret? The thoughts ran through her mind in that moment as she began to rummage through her purse to locate her AirPods. She put them into her ears and waited to hear her father's voice. She wanted to be just as messy, but she promised both Delilah and Reign she wouldn't say anything.

"What's going on, sweet pea?" The sound of her father's voice instantly pulled her from her thoughts as a smirk graced her face. Sno was the only man who had that effect on her. Not only did she love him, but she admired him, not only as her father but as a man as well.

"Hey, Daddy," Heaven said, sighing as she pulled down the sun visor. She began playing with her hair, running her long nails through her blonde weave as she stared at her own reflection in the mirror.

"What's wrong? Did you see your apartment yet?"

"First of all, I want to let you know how much I truly appreciate you. I love you so much, Daddy. Your parenting is impeccable," she smiled. "I have not seen my apartment yet, but I'm sure it is beautiful."

"Nothing but the best for my sweet pea," Sno announced honestly. "I had Jayla go over there and decorate for me."

"Oh really? Well, I'm not worried at all. If Jayla touched it, I know my crib is off the chain. Hopefully, I'll be on my way there soon."

"What's the hold up? I know you landed by now."

"Esha had to pick something up from her in laws."

"Oh yeah? What neighborhood are you in?" Sno asked.

"I don't know. It looks terrible over here though."

"It looks terrible?" he inquired. His voice was full of worry as he tried to figure out her location. "Are you inside a house?"

"No, I'm sitting in the car... I told Esha..." Her words drifted off when she turned her head to look out the driver side window. "Oh my God," she whispered under her breath as a black BMW X5 pulled on the side of Esha's truck to parallel park. She squinted her eyes, knowing they weren't deceiving her as she stared at the side of a face she couldn't and would never forget, considering the face was identical to her daughter's. Heaven pushed the visor back down and afterwards, looked inside her bag to retrieve her lip stain, forgetting she was on the phone with Sno.

"You either need to get out the car or call your friend and tell her to hurry up. It's not safe to sit in cars out there." Heaven was silent as she pursed her lips and applied her Mac. "Heaven, did you hear me?" he asked.

"Yes, Father!"

"I know I'm a far way from Chicago, but don't be hardheaded, Heaven. I would've felt better if Derrick had went with you," he said, voice full of authority.

"Calm down. She'll be out in a few minutes." She sucked her teeth. "And Derrick would've just been in the way. Speaking of Derrick..." Heaven began, but Sno cut the conversation short.

"Heaven, get out the car and call me back once you're home. We can talk about Derrick then."

"Daddy, I am okay."

"No, you're not. I didn't send none of my niggas out there with you. I was tryna let you be an adult." He told her a half truth. It was true Sno didn't send any of his people to Chicago with Heaven, but he made sure she had some type of protection. He asked Dre to have one of his people look after Heaven.

Heaven sucked her teeth. "I am an adult, Daddy. I don't need anyone following me and watching my every move."

"I know you're an adult, sweet pea. Just get out the car and call me as soon as you get home. As a matter of fact, FaceTime me, so I can see how Jayla set everything up."

"Okay, Daddy," she said in a whiny tone. "Talk to you later."

"Alright. I love you."

"I love you too." Heaven hung up. She knew she had seen the profile of Kash's face, so before she stepped out, she looked at the side mirror.

As soon as she did, she saw Kash step from the front passenger side of the truck. His size thirteen Jordans touched the pavement, and she couldn't help but to stare. Stuck in place, Heaven studied everything about him. Kash's clothing was a pair of black and white basketball shorts. His upper body was bare with a black shirt thrown over his shoulder. His brown hair was in a fade, the same exact brown as Kamelia's. His almost full beard was just as brown as his fade. His skin was sun kissed, as if he had been outside all day.

Still, he looked exactly as he did over five years ago on the night she met him. At this point, her mouth was wide open as she was on the verge of opening the car door. He was so tall that she didn't even notice the female that stepped out the truck behind him until she ran up on the side of him and grabbed his hand.

"Who the fuck is that bitch?" she asked no one in particular. She was about five feet and four inches tall. She looked mixed with slanted eyes and long, beautiful, shiny, black hair that hung down to her waist. She was absolutely gorgeous. Her face, her brown skin, even her body was beautiful, still Heaven was unbothered. She was here on a mission, and little Miss Slanted Eyes wasn't going to stand in the way of that. It took everything in Heaven not to get out the truck and act an ass. She had to admit she was a little envious. Heaven was sure the girl had children. Her hips were spread too wide not to. And she was more than sure Kash was playing daddy but had never laid an eye on his own child.

Instantly, her body began to tremble, especially her hands. She was upset. Angry tears began to run down her face, but she quickly wiped them away. She looked down into her phone and called Esha. The phone rang a couple times before she answered.

"I'm on my way out right now."

"Please hurry up. I can't do this shit."

"Do what shit?"

"Just please hurry up, Esha." Heaven hung up as Esha's driver side door swung open. Heaven jumped. She was afraid for her life.

"Yo', what's up, Heaven G?" Lance said excitedly. They hadn't seen each other in person in well over five years, but they spoke often whenever Esha was around him while she was on the phone with Heaven. Just a quick hey or what's up. Nothing personal or unusual.

"Hey, Lance." She smiled, holding her chest "You scared the shit outta me."

"My bad, man. I thought shorty had a mufuckin' nigga in the car."

"Do I look like a nigga to you?" Heaven frowned while laughing.

"Naw, man. I just saw movement in the car. I was ready to air this mufucka out."

"Chicago shit, huh?" She laughed.

"Nah, real life shit. How you been though?" he asked. Without allowing her to answer, he looked up as Kash and Asia passed the truck and began walking towards the house. "Aye, K..."

"No, don't call him over here," she said, stopping Lance in mid octave as she yanked at his drenched basketball jersey. "Don't do that." She frowned. He was clearly with his woman. In the past, the past being only hours ago, Heaven swore she was ready to fight Kash and whoever if she saw him with another woman. However, she didn't want to look foolish or feel foolish. She didn't know if he still felt the same way about her as he felt in the past, and she would much rather make a fool of herself when they were alone, instead of in public.

"Man, that girl don't mean shit to him," he said assuredly as both Kash and Asia stopped walking in mid stride.

"Who is that, G?" Kash yelled curiously, gesturing his head in a what's up motion. "Is that Esha?" He removed his hand from Asia's. "I'ma meet you in the house." He pointed Asia in the direction of Lance's mother's home.

"Okay." She walked away as Kash stood there, making sure she was inside before he walked over to the truck. The windows were still raised, so he couldn't see who he was inside, still was curious. He tapped thewindow.

"You see what you did." Heaven's eyes widened, and her heart began to beat nervously. Just the thought of being this close to Kash made her feel weak.

"Heaven, just let the nigga see you," Lance said, encouraging her. He wanted to see how both would react to being in each other's presence after all these years.

"Heaven?" Kash asked. He yanked at the door handle, but Heaven had quickly secured the lock.

"No, fuck him." Heaven was stubborn. She refused to let her window down. "He has a whole bitch with him. He doesn't need to see me."

"Open the door, Heaven," Kash said, still holding on to the door handle.

"Go away, Kashmir!"

"What?" He frowned, looking as if something smelled foul. "Open the fucking door."

"Lance, tell your friend to go away."

"Man, y'all too old to be playing games. I'm not in this shit," Lance said; however, he still pressed the key button to unlock the doors.

Heaven locked them right back.

"Lance, please stop. I don't want to talk to him right now, not in front of everyone. And I definitely don't want to fight his little girlfriend over what's technically mine," she said, taking a breath and sitting back in her seat. She looked out her window into Kash's face. She could see him clearly, but he had to squint and press his face up against the glass to see her. Her heart was racing so fast. Heaven felt anxious and weak. She didn't realize it before, but now that she was seeing him and his eagerness to see her, she knew she still loved him, and she knew his feelings had to be mutual.

"Heaven, open the door," Kash said. "I don't want nothing from you. I just wanna see you, shorty. I need to talk to you."

"No!" she yelled. "Fuck you, Kash. I still look like that sixteen-year-old girl you left five years ago. I had to go through my pregnancy and take care of our baby alone," she said, trying to make him feel bad, knowing she never had to do anything alone because her father was there every step of the way.

She knew what she came to Chicago to do, but she just couldn't. She'd forgiven him a long time ago but seeing him with Asia pissed her off. So, she used their past to get under his skin. In her mind, she could deal with him moving on. She was able to make idle threats, but seeing the shit was hurting her, and she couldn't explain why.

"Man, I'm not tryna hear none of that shit. Open the door."

Lance just shook his head as he watched Heaven yell and scream. He then wondered why Kash didn't just walk around to the driver's side, seeing as though the door was wide open.

"Lance, G, unlock the door."

"Lance, don't touch that fuckin' lock."

Behind the tinted glass, she scowled, wishing Esha would hurry up. She needed time and space to get her mind right.

"Heaven, you got me out here begging you. I don't have to beg a female for shit, and I'm out here begging you to talk to me."

"Then don't beg me. Just go the fuck away. Go in there with your bitch!" she yelled. "She looked pissed."

"Asia did look pissed, bro," Lance chimed in as he watched her step back onto the porch to watch the show with the rest of the block. People began to step from their homes and crowd around the altercation.

"Fuck Asia." Right now, she wasn't a factor. Heaven was the woman who bore his child. In his heart, he knew he fucked up a long time ago. Heaven deserved an apology. She deserved more than that, and he was ready to give her more. It was not necessarily a relationship because he was already dealing with someone else; however, he was ready to be there for both Heaven and Kamelia. "It shouldn't take all this, Heaven."

"It shouldn't, and five years ago, it wouldn't have, but now, it's fuck you." Sitting back in her seat, she folded her arms defiantly. "I don't want to talk."

"You know what?" Kash said in a calm tone before throwing a hard jab. His fist crashed against the sturdy, dark glass so hard that he almost shattered his wrist. Still, the window didn't break, and the adrenaline that flowed through him in that moment masked the sharp pain that shot through his knuckles. Normally, Kash was calm and laidback. His demeanor was very serene. But Heaven was testing him with her defiance. He felt entitled to her because they shared something deeper than sex. Kamelia was the proof of that.

"Aaaahhh!" Heaven jumped and screamed. Kash was acting a little psycho. "Kash! Stop!" Her heart raced erratically. She presumed he didn't take rejection very well. It showed in his actions in this moment. The ooooouuuus, daaaammmms, and that nigga is wildin' caused Esha and Asia to step on the porch.

"Aye, man. What the fuck you doing?" Lance ran from the driver's side to Kash and grabbed him up but not before he hit the window again. "G, you can't make shorty talk to you. Esha gon' beat yo' overly emotional ass, man."

"My bad, G." He took a deep breath and looked at his hand. "Esha know I will get her window fixed if I break it."

"That's besides the point, bro. Look at this shit. All these mufuckas out here watching you act a fool. G, this ain't for you."

"Man, fuck these people," he said.

Esha stood next to Asia on the porch with their

mouths wide open. Esha had no idea who Asia was, but she was sure Asia was here with Kash. So, she looked at Asia with her nose turned up. She was a dumb ass, standing on the porch, watching her man act a fool over another female.

"Couldn't be me!" she stated as she descended the stairs with baby Lance on her hip. "What the hell is going on?" Seeing Lance now standing in between Kash and the truck, she knew he had done something.

"Kash, what the fuck are you doing to my friend and my truck? And who is this dumb bitch you got on mymother-in-law's stoop?"

"Bitch, who are you?" Asia rebutted.

"Man, Heaven, just let the window down and talk to this nigga before you get some shit started out here!"

"Started with who?" Esha asked. "I'm not thinking about that girl. While her man is over here, all in my friend's face, that bitch is on the porch like a pussy. I bet Kash told her to stand her ditzy ass up there, and just like a puppy, she did."

"I got your bitch!" Asia yelled from where she stood. Asia didn't really want to cause a scene, especially after what happened the night before with Nadia. She needed to tuck that ghetto, ratchet, smart mouth attitude away. That way Kash would see her as a good girl and not a crazy bitch. She figured he would love her for being the perfect woman. But what Asia didn't know was that he didn't mind the ratchet shit when it came from the right person. So, she stood there and took the insults from Esha. And she stood there and watched her man go crazy over some random chick.

"Girl, boo!" Esha taunted, laughing.

"Esha, shut the fuck up and put my son in the car. I told you about doing all that extra shit." His voice was serious and demanding.

"Watch it, Lance!"

"I ain't gotta watch shit. Put my son in the car and stay out their business."

"Nah uhn, Lance, you doing too much. But I'ma put him in the truck and mind my own business after I say this. Kash, you bring this bucket head ass bitch over here to flaunt around in front of my friend and expect my friend to roll her window down and talk to you? Hell naw, friend, don't be goofy like that bitch over there. If it's fuck that nigga, then that's what it is." She walked to the back door. "Unlock the door, Heaven."

As she said that, Lance moved out of Kash's way. That was his opportunity to talk to Heaven.

"Esha, stay out their business before I choke yo' ass."

"I said I was done, damn." She put her baby inside, and Kash swiftly snatched the front door open before Heaven could even think to lock it.

"That's how you do that shit, my nigga," Lance laughed.

"So, it's fuck me?" Kash asked, and Heaven took in a deep breath, placing her Dior sunglasses on to cover her eyes. "That's what you're on?" he asked, taking the glasses back off her face. She looked up at him, in his eyes, as he looked down at her. The energy and sparks between the two were undeniable. This was one thing she feared, falling so deeply in love with him all over again without getting to the bottom of why things ended the way they did in the first place.

She wanted to reach up, touch his face, and kiss his lips, just to make sure he was real. Instead, the two were silent as they looked into each other's eyes, studying one another. Kash awaited Heaven's answer to his question as Heaven tried not to be nervous. She wanted to say, 'No, Kash, it's never been fuck you. I love you,' but she couldn't. He had moved on, so yes, it was fuck him.

"Yes, Kash, it's fuck you. Now move so I can go." She spoke harshly and adamantly. Her face was scowled, and her attitude was peeved. She didn't mean any part of anything she was saying, still her tone was convincing.

Esha stood there, eves dropping as she buckled baby Lance into his car seat. She wanted to chime in on the conversation and tell Heaven to stop being a bitch towards the man she flew 1,000 miles to see. She shook her head and pursed her lips. She could understand how her friend felt. However, she did warn her before it even got to this point. Years ago, when Heaven told Esha her real age, she tried to tell her to dead anything she had going on with Kashmir, but Heaven didn't listen. Now, here they were. Esha knew Heaven understood that part, and she knew Heaven was only upset right now because Kash had moved on. Looking at Heaven's face, she could tell she'd come to her own conclusion on Kash's situation and relationship. Even with that said, it was a known fact that Kash was a ladies' man. Hell, even Lance was a ladies' man, but Esha was immune to his doggish ways, plus he took care of their son. Kash and Lance were two niggas who couldn't help themselves when it came to females, still Kash and Lance were not the same.

"You sure that's what you want?" Kash asked. His feelings were a little hurt. No woman could or had ever fixed their mouth to deny him.

"Yes, Kashmir." She tried to grab the door handle, but Kash pushed her hand back. "Do not touch me, Kash."

"Don't touch you?"

"You heard me, Kashmir. Don't touch me… Move."

"You got shit fucked up, Heaven." He gripped her chin with his thumb and forefinger. He didn't play games with anyone nor did he tolerate disrespect. So, his touch was commanding and slightly forceful.

Shit! Heaven thought as she looked into his eyes. Him touching her felt good. Damn, bitch, stop playing with this man. You love him. You want him in Kamelia's life. Don't push him away. She moaned under her breath as her chest heaved up and down.

"Don't touch me." She moved her face from his grasp.

"Esha, come here. Let them talk!" Lance yelled out.

"I am. Damn, Lance. Give me a second." He already knew she was being nosey. This was like an episode of an urban soap opera. Esha wished she had a bottle of wine to go with this live performance because Heaven was definitely putting on an act. Esha knew how she really felt though. Considering how Heaven felt about Kash, she knew this here wasn't it. Esha had a few words for Heaven, but she was going to save her scolding for later when they were alone.

After locking her son in, she attempted to walk away, but Heaven asked her not to.

"He's leaving, Esha. Let's go, friend." With one last look into Kash's eyes, she turned her face and stared straight ahead. "Have a good day, Kash."

"We about to leave, bae." Esha slammed the back door and ran over to Lance. She wrapped her arms around him and kissed him while he palmed her ass.

"I'm about to take Heaven home. I'm sure she wants to unpack and get settled in… I'm gonna help her for a little while, and then I will be home."

"Aight." He pecked her lips again. "I'll see you in a few hours."

"Okay." She walked in the direction of the truck while Lance walked to his mother's steps and began to climb them. He didn't know where the crowd went, but in the midst of everything, everyone dispersed.

"That's how you feel, Miss Wright?" His voice was so laidback that even her name rolling off his tongue harmonized. Still, she remained silent. "I just wanted to see how our daughter is doing," Kash said, clearing his throat, watching as Esha climbed in on the driver's side.

"Oh! She's our daughter now?" Heaven smirked.

"What you mean now?" He frowned. "Where is Baby K… I mean Kamelia?"

"She's at home. Where else would she be?" she responded snidely, and Esha laughed.

"Stop doing him like that."

"It's cool. I understand," he said, chuckling himself.

"Kash!" Asia said his name loudly; however, he was stuck in a trance, focused on Heaven's lips as she talked sassily to him.

"Kash, your little girlfriend is on her way over here, and if she touches anything on or inside my truck, I'ma beat the brakes off her ass," Esha threatened.

Kash let out an exasperated breath, wanting to say more to Heaven, but he didn't want a confrontation between Esha and Asia. Esha was mean as hell, and Asia was mentally dysfunctional. And if Asia was walking over to him, she was coming to fight.

"Tame your beast, Kashmir," Heaven said, cocking her head to the side to look at Asia.

"Man," Kash chuckled. "Don't leave yet. Let me tame her as you say, and I will be right back." He hadn't forgotten Asia was there. She just didn't matter at the moment. Kash didn't like drama, and he'd be damned if he was in the middle of it. He closed Heaven's door and turned to look at Asia as she approached him.

"I tried to hold her back, G!" Lance yelled, shrugging his shoulders.

Heaven shook her head as Kash walked away. Intently, she watched as he gripped Asia's chin, and she knew they had to be in love. She couldn't hear what they were saying, but from their hand gestures and body movements, the conversation between the two seemed to be pretty intense and passion driven. There was nowhere for her to compete.

"This was not what I came to Chicago for." Seeing him with another bitch was not something she could deal with. She looked over at Esha with saddened eyes and bawled.

"Well, boo, I told you way before y'all ever fucked not to fuck with him like that. But I'm not here to throw anything in your face." She grabbed Heaven's hand. "Look, if it'll make you feel better, we can get out this truck and go beat her ass."

"No, I'm not fighting over no nigga. I know better than that. I have a whole fiancé at home. I shouldn't even be feeling like this."

"I can just beat her ass. Hell, that'll make me feel better."

"No."

"Well, how long you about to be crying over this nigga? You have a whole fiancé, right? So, do what the hell you came here to do and shut the fuck up," Esha said, and Heaven looked at her like she had lost her mind. "What? I love you, Heaven, and I'm going to be here for you no matter what. But I hate that crying shit. We should be out here having fun, not sulking. You're too beautiful to be crying over a nigga you're not going to fight over."

"I'm not allowed to feel, Esha?"

"Yes, you are, but shit, don't feel that shit in front of the world. It's been five years. He moved on; hell, you moved on. But I can guarantee you he loves you."

Heaven sighed. Growing up, Anika taught her how to use men. Not for money but for love and attention. She'd never told her how it would feel to get played herself. She also tried to be ahead of the game. So, this had her heart bruised. Everything Esha said made perfectly good sense, so she needed to get away and give herself time to recuperate. She planned to revisit her plan in a few days. "Let's just go."

"Are you sure?"

"Yes." Blinking back tears, Heaven nodded her head.

"Look, I didn't mean to hurt your feelings, I just…"

"It's okay. I needed to hear that. Let's just go, friend."

"Okay, my love. Let's go." Esha started up her truck, and Heaven looked out the window at Kash as she drove away.

***

"It better be a famous bitch in that truck, Kashmir." Asia pointed in his face. "Because you are definitely about to make me bust this bitch head. I let you stand over here and disrespect me long enough."

"You ain't busting shit, shorty," he said, moving her finger from his face. "This situation don't have nothing to do with you. You know I'm not into all that drama shit, Asia." He walked up on her and gripped her chin, looking into her eyes.

"Who is that in the car, Kash? And you let that tall, lanky ass bitch talk crazy to me," she said as she began to tear up. Her tears were fake, but she wanted Kash to feel bad about his actions.

"That's my daughter's mother."

"Your daughter's mother? Wait a minute, nigga," she said, raising her voice and pointing her finger in his face once again. "I'm just finding out about your daughter today, and now you're beating down windows and shit, trying to see your bitch ass baby mama. What the hell are we doing here?" she said.

Kash chuckled and shook his head. "It's not even like that with us."

"Oh, no? Then why am I standing out here looking like your fool while you beg her to talk to you?"

"I don't know, Asia. You tell me. She don't even live in Chicago, man. You getting loud and making yourself look foolish for nothing. I'm out here with you, and that's all that should matter. If you want to leave because you feel like I'm making you look stupid, by all means go. Either way, I need to have a conversation with the mother of my child."

"You have to do it now, in front of me?"

"I can't pacify your insecurities, Asia. So, either go in Miss Roberts's crib and wait on me or leave."

Asia's nostrils flared as she looked Kash in his eyes. She was pissed, but she needed to make sure Heaven knew he was all hers. Whatever they had in the past was done and over with.

"Okay, well, give me a kiss before I go," she demanded with a cute smirk on her face. Cocking her head to the side, she raised one eyebrow.

"You need me to kiss you to prove what?" he asked.

"Nothing." She stiffened her neck. She was lying, and Kash knew it. He shook his head and let out a breath. He wrapped his arms around her waist as she wrapped her arms around his neck and forced her lips on his. He gave in to her weak ass demand. Nothing passionate, just a few pecks before Asia was satisfied. She removed her arms, and so did he.

"You good now?" he asked, looking down at her. She smiled and nodded her head yes.

"I'll be in Miss Roberts's house, waiting on you. Tell your baby mama I said hey."

Kash turned his back to Asia, and she stuck her

tongue out. Now that Kash had given the entire block a show, she was happy.

But as soon as he began to walk to the truck, Esha pulled off. Kash sighed, watching Esha's truck pull away from the curb. He hung his head. He had no way to get in contact with Heaven, and he knew she wouldn't dare step a foot back on Lance's mother's block, not after the way he ambushed her. He also knew Esha would never give him her information.

"Fuck!"

TEN

Anika sat in her car, parked across the street from Heaven's home with her seat laid back and her head resting up against the headrest. She had been sitting out there for a few hours now, watching Heaven's home, waiting for Derrick to get back from dropping Heaven off at the airport. Even after he returned home, she remained outside, conflicted about everything. She deserved happiness. She also deserved love, both of which she only had with Sno. Anika didn't even know how to love her children correctly because they were created with a man her heart didn't know how to let go of; however, his heart gave up on her a long time ago.

She started up the ignition on her car. Almost instantly, air whooshed inside through the vents, and Tank's Maybe I Deserve played through the speaker. It was no coincidence that this song played seeing as though this was the last song she'd turned to before her car turned off. She usually liked rap music, but the wine she'd been drinking since this morning had her in her feelings. Anika was an emotional mess. Her face was red, and her eyes were swollen from crying. The day before, she tried to tell Heaven about everything she was going through, but every time they interacted with each other, things seemed to go left. In the past, she'd had a personal conversation with Derrick, and she looked at him like a son. So, today, she showed up at their home with every intention to feel better.

With thoughts of her life running crazy in her mind, she felt as if she was going insane. Tears ran from her eyes as she gripped a bottle of wine in her hand. It was only ten in the morning, too early to be drinking, but she was depressed. This really had to be it for her. She'd been through plenty emotions in her life, but depression was the worst. Anika was ghetto as hell, always the loudest person in the room, but she also considered herself classy. Never would she be caught looking a mess with a bonnet on her head and dressed in a bathrobe with only her panties and bra underneath or drinking liquor out of a liquor bottle, but right now, she didn't know any other way to deal with her current predicament. She still loved Sno, but after he finds out what she's been keeping a secret for months now, she knew he would cut her off indefinitely. She knew it would only be a matter of time before he found out there was a very strong possibility that Delilah wasn't his daughter. The other man was asking for a paternity test.

Now, she needed to come up with a masterplan. Anika needed to have another baby with Sno in order to keep him funding her lifestyle for the sake of their babies. The day she snuck into KeKe's home and had sex with Sno while he was sleeping, that was exactly what she planned to do. However, it didn't work out that way.

Anika inclined her seat back into position, took a sip from her Pinto Noir, and drove into the driveway. She came to an abrupt stop, killed the engine, and stepped out with her wine bottle in her hand as she pulled her robe closed. She took another sip as she approached the door.

***

As soon as Derrick returned home from dropping Heaven off at the airport, he retrieved his rolling tray, cigar, and weed from his closet. He quickly unwound. Taking his shirt and shoes off, he took a seat on the bed and turned the television on to the channel five news before he proceeded to roll up. Focusing his attention on the task at hand, he licked the brown paper, making sure it was nice and damp before he used his fingers to break down the cigar and afterwards emptied it. On the inside, he was fucked up. He felt just like that cigar. Empty. He didn't know how he allowed Heaven to take this trip alone. He was confused with her wanting to go alone. He understood and agreed that Kamelia should know who her biological father was, but Heaven had left her behind in Atlanta. She'd left everyone she loved behind in Atlanta to find Kash. He was engaged to Heaven, so this should've been a journey they embarked on together. Still, he had to trust her. He knew she was smart. She wouldn't do anything stupid to jeopardize their relationship, especially not with a man who left her for dead when she was pregnant. Clearly, he didn't know her that well.

Picking up a tightly sealed ziplock bag full of spiky, leafy green that smelled rank, he took a sniff and frowned. Derrick had plans to get real fucked up and afterwards get his day started. He unzipped the bag and meticulously, he began laying as much weed as his cigar would hold inside. After successfully rolling a fat blunt, he took the rest of his clothes off and went into the bathroom to take a shower.

It took him all of ten minutes before he stepped out and wrapped a towel around his waist. Hearing the doorbell ring over and over, he had no time to dry off or get dressed. Still soaked and wet, he made his way downstairs to the front door.

Ding Dong! He looked through the peephole and quickly snatched the door open, seeing Anika standing there in a bathrobe that hung wide open, exposing her underwear, and a bottle of red wine in her hand. He looked at her with a confused expression on his face. He knew she was mentally unstable, but this was unusual. He had never seen her this way before.

The entire situation was awkward. Him in nothing but a towel around his waist and her half naked.

"Is everything okay?" he asked as he looked her up and down. She was barefoot, and her face was tear streaked. She seemed to be having a mental crisis.

"Yes, I'm wonderful," she lied. "I just stopped by to talk to Heaven before she leaves for Chicago."

"Heaven left already. You didn't get the group message?" Anika put her phone up to her face to unlock it. She did get Heaven's message, but she had to play it off.

"I don't have a message from her." She raised one brow as she pretended to look for Heaven's message.

"Well, she left a couple hours ago,"

"Damn." Anika sucked her teeth. Tears began to pour from her eyes and ran down her face as she said, "I tried to make it before she left. I need her to know that I love her."

"Heaven knows you love her. What happened, Anika? Why are you outside like this? Where are your clothes and your shoes?" he inquired as she lifted the wine bottle and took a swig from it.

"Fuck clothes and shoes, I need to see my child." She was deliriously putting on an act. Anika already knew Heaven was not there. She was sitting right outside her home when she left. Still, she wanted some attention from anyone who gave Heaven attention, and she knew Sno was not going to deal with her bullshit. Plus, Derrick understood her and her illness.

"She's not here." He frowned, pulling her robe closed. He pulled the belt together and tied it. "Come in." Stepping to the side, Anika smiled widely as she staggered inside. Derrick shook his head as she tried to balance herself. He peeped his head outside before slamming the door shut.

"Derrick." Anika said his name as she led the way in the direction of the living room.

"Yeah." He followed behind her, fixing his towel, making sure it was securing his lower body.

"I need to lay down. I feel so sick." She took a long, deep, intoxicated breath.

"Yeah, lay right here on the couch. Do you need some water or anything?"

"No, Derrick, I don't need any water." Seductively, she took a seat on the couch, set her bottle of wine on the floor, untied her robe, and laid back. Her robe fell completely open, and Derrick turned his head to look in the opposite direction. But the quick glance he got of her body made his dick jump. Anika's body was beautiful. She didn't have any stretch marks besides the few that were on the sides of her ass. Her stomach was flat, her breasts sat up, thanks to the wired bra she had on, and her vagina was fat. Derrick managed to see all of that in those few split seconds.

"Aye, I'ma run upstairs real quick and put some clothes on." He said that with his back still turned towards her.

"Derrick, stop acting shy," she slurred, laughing as she hit his leg. "Look at me," she seductively requested.

"What size do you wear? Maybe I can bring you something from Heaven's closet to put on." he asked without looking at her.

"I'm fine. I don't need any clothes on." She began to pull her robe closed.

Derrick was uncomfortable, and it showed. Without another word, he walked away. Once he entered the bedroom, he quickly put on a pair of boxers and blue jean shorts. The entire time, the awkwardness of he and Anika's encounter ran through his mind.

She's lucky I'm not a disrespectful nigga, he thought. He imagined how Heaven would feel knowing that her mother was trying to seduce him. They already had a love hate relationship, so, in that moment, he knew he wouldn't tell her. Still, he picked his phone up and dialed her number. He knew she wasn't going to answer, still he called her anyways, just in case. After getting her voicemail, he sat silent on the phone for a few seconds before hanging up.

Picking up his rolled blunt from the bed, he lit it, puffing it as the brown tip turned a fiery red and gray.

After what just happened a few minutes ago, he needed this. Instantly, his nerves began to calm.

Five minutes later, he was a little high. With his brain on go, he was laid up against the headboard with the remote in one hand, his blunt in the other, and his face in a scowl as he watched the midday news, analyzing the entire segment.

"Niggas ain't worried about no mufuckin' covid," he mumbled. "I'll die before I let any mufucka stick me wit' a needle. The government know who to play wit'." He was on a rampage. The weed had him very woke. Derrick was so far in his one-on-one conversation with himself that he had forgotten all about Anika. That was until he heard her heavy footsteps walking around upstairs, and he heard her loud, country voice calling his name.

"Derrick!" she yelled.

"Fuck." He sat up from the headboard. Scooting to the edge of the bed, he planted his feet on the floor.
"I'm in here!" he said hesitantly.

She came stumbling into the room. Before taking a step all the way inside, she stood there at the doorway and smiled. "What you doing?" She sighed and walked over to the bed. "I wanted to talk to you, but my head is spinning so fucking bad. I probably need to lay back down." She looked at the bed suggestively.

"Here, sit down." He motioned to the side of him.

"Okay." She took a seat and looked at him as he occupied his eyes with the TV's remote.

"So, what do I owe the pleasure, Anika? I know you know Heaven is gone to Chicago."

Anika bent over while still seated. She felt a little embarrassed. Derrick was right. With her head in her hands, she almost fell off the bed.

"Be careful." Derrick put his cigar into his mouth and grabbed Anika's shoulder, pulling her back up. "What's really going on?" he asked and raised his hands in surprise as Anika's head fell onto his bare chest.

"Derrick!" She cried dramatically. "Heaven is going to hate me forever after she finds out what I have done."

"What did you do?" He frowned and removed his cigar from his mouth. Rubbing the top of her silk bonnet awkwardly, he tried to understand what she was going through.

"I have no one else to confide in, Derrick. But this shit is weighing so heavy on me."

"Sit up." He grabbed her shoulders and held them as she sat up. He was relieved she was no longer laying on him. He looked at her in her eyes, which were red and puffy. "Just say it. What did you do?"

"Do you promise not to say anything? Will you let me tell Heaven and Sno myself?" she asked as they both stared at each other.

"Yeah, mane. It's your business to tell."

"Ok… Sno…" She closed her eyes. "He's not Delilah's father. Well, I don't know if he's her father or not, but there is a strong possibility he isn't," she said through a hiccup.

"Say word?" His eyes grew in size. "I mean, what makes you feel that he isn't?"

"Was that really a question, Derrick? What else would make me feel that way?"

Derrick chuckled. He had to agree. That was a dumb question.

"After me and Sno broke up years ago, I started dealing with this nigga from the east side. Honestly, I just wanted to get back at Demarco for leaving me. But me being with other men didn't bother him. Demarco and I continued to fuck. I couldn't tell Bully that I was still dealing with Sno. Sno's name is big in Georgia, and Bully has a little clout. But he's a good guy. He took care of me and Heaven."

"So, Bully stepped in when Sno stopped providing?" he asked, confused.

"No, Sno never stopped providing for Heaven. He

even took great care of Delilah when she was born although he has his doubts."

"Damn. That's fucked up. But drinking like this won't solve the problem, Anika."

"I know." She laid her head back on Derrick's chest, and he embraced her. "I really don't know how to tell them. Heaven already hates me. I don't even know if I should tell them."

"I can't tell you what to do, but everyone involved deserves to know the truth. We all make mistakes. Nobody will hold your past against you," Derrick said, but he had no idea how untrue his statement was.

"Thank you, Derrick. I needed that." She sat up and retrieved the remote. "What's good on TV?" Standing up, she walked to the foot of the bed and laid across it on her stomach.

"Make yourself comfortable," he chuckled, and Anika did just that. She began flipping through the channels as she made herself comfortable.

After their conversation, Derrick relit his cigar and took his spot back up against the headboard. He felt good knowing he was able to help their situation. After smoking the rest of his weed, within a few minutes, he was knocked out.

He woke up a little after 2pm to Anika laying on his chest, snuggled up against him, and his arm wrapped around her.

To be continued…

187